Julia Clarke

Brought up with her twin sister in the 1960s, Julia Clarke left school at sixteen. Having decided she wanted to be a writer at the age of seven, she wrote her first novel in 1987, after a circuitous route which included spells as a nanny, librarian, barmaid, cook at a remote Scottish country mansion, drama teacher, actress, theatre usherette, stage manager, cashier, wardrobe mistress and secretary to an astrologer. She has since had six adult novels published, as well as several short stories. After travelling widely in Afghanistan and India, Julia married and had two children. She now lives on a farm in North Yorkshire with a dog, rabbits and hens. Her hobbies include theatre, music, walking, reading, travel and cooking.

THE Starling Tree

by Julia Clarke

An imprint of HarperCollins*Publishers*

First published in Great Britain by CollinsFlamingo in 2001
CollinsFlamingo is an imprint of HarperCollins*Publishers* Ltd,
77-85 Fulham Palace Road, Hammersmith,
London W6 8JB

The HarperCollins website address is
www.**fire**and**water**.com

13 5 7 9 10 8 6 4 2

Text copyright © Julia Clarke 2001

ISBN 0 00 710514-2

Printed and bound in Great Britain by
Omnia Books Ltd, Glasgow G64

To my homies – Bethany, Matt and Mike – with love

1

It was awful the day our school hit the news – newspaper men arrived first and then the television crews. They arrived in huge blue and grey vans, and out of these vans spewed tired-looking men in faded jeans and robust girls in hiking boots. Bluebottle called it a media circus, but it didn't look like a circus to me. It looked like the end of the rest of my life.

We'd had the local papers the week before – snobby girls with floppy hair and boys in tweed jackets, hanging around the gates, asking people for quotes. Some of the gobby kids, like Kerry-Ann and Miranda, had been out there telling tales about riots in the corridors and knife attacks. And that was how it started.

But now we are news. Big news. We are going to be on the telly. Kerry-Ann and Miranda, who have been leaning out of the window and screeching at everyone, are now in the bog putting on lipstick and trying to sing in harmony.

'Want to sing with us, Fawn?' Miranda asks me, as they finish the song.

Shaking my head despairingly, I ask: 'What do you think is going to happen? That we'll be spotted by a talent scout and become a new girlie band? No chance! That lot outside are going to put Meadowlea School on the map as the biggest dustbin school in the whole wide world. We'll carry the stigma of being Meadowlea pupils like a tattoo on our foreheads for the rest of our lives.'

'Oh gawd,' Miranda says, rolling her big brown eyes. 'She's swallowed the bleeding dictionary again.' They link arms, giggle, and begin to sing again.

I go in search of Adam. Sometimes I think he is the only sane person in the whole of the Universe. He is hiding out in the library – the room with some tatty books and an Encyclopaedia Britannica published in 1959 which passes for a library and study centre at Meadowlea. He is working on an English assignment. Because we are alone he kisses me on the lips and I sit on his knee, wrapping my arms around his neck and getting comfort from the warmth and nearness of him. Adam always smells lovely. His mum is a wash freak and makes him wear clean clothes every day, as well as bathing in the evening and showering in the morning. His hair is tightly curled honey-blond, like a teddy bear. He's gorgeous.

'Have you seen it? ITV and the BBC...' I say miserably.

'All the thick-heads think it's great.'

'They've been around the back, filming the broken windows,' Adam reports with a shrug.

'It will freak my Pa out. He's been batting on about a full moon in Aries and a configuration between Uranus and Pluto. He said something momentous was going to happen.'

Adam kisses me again, but he is preoccupied and eases me gently off his lap. It's obvious he wants to get back to his essay. Adam is the biggest swot at Meadowlea and I'm the second biggest. Apart from us, no one in our year seems very keen on working.

'It'll be all right. Nobody will take any notice of us,' he says.

'But we'll have to put Meadowlea School down on our job applications – how will it look?' I ask desperately. I'd had trouble getting a weekend job. One bloke at Netto had said to me openly: 'We don't use Meadowlea kids, they pinch things.' It's all right for Adam – his step-dad has his own business and gives Adam holiday work. He gets to wear blue overalls and go out pretending to be a plumber's mate.

Adam isn't listening to me and so I decide to shut up. 'I'm nicking off home,' I say to Adam, and he turns around and kisses me again.

'See you tonight. About seven-thirty. Usual place.'

It's easy to get out of school. I sneak through the caretaker's door and skirt around the edge of the playground. Miss Harbottle, who is wearing more make-up than usual, is standing on the front steps giving an interview to the cameras. She is happily oblivious to all the nerdy little kids standing behind her pulling faces and doing V signs.

Why do I get the feeling that everyone else in the world is enjoying this apart from me? It's as if the teachers are glorying in the fact that they have to teach such awful kids. They walk around looking proud and resigned – like war heroes about to be presented with their medals.

My shoulders are hunched with misery as I walk quickly away from the school. Some Victorian builder with an evil sense of humour named the school Meadowlea. It is stuck like an enormous pimple on the windiest hillside in the city, and is miles from anything remotely resembling a meadow or a field. Instead it is hemmed in by factories, mills and the poor little houses built in the olden days to house the workers.

Walking down the steep hill, under the clear blue spring sky, I can see bright patches of green on the far hillside. That is the posh side of town, where people have gardens. Our side of the valley doesn't have many trees, and my route home takes me along empty roads of old blackstone back-to-back houses. A lot of them are boarded up. The whole area was meant to be redeveloped years ago, but after the people moved out, the streets kind of got forgotten. Now it's a place where sticky-heads gather to sniff glue and packs of stray dogs run wild.

I'm not really meant to walk home alone, even when it's

light. But Ginna, my bro, is off in town with Spider and the rest of the creeps he hangs about with now. I sigh as I walk, because it's dreadful not knowing where Ginna is and thinking that he might be getting into trouble. Since the school gave up trying to stop truanting, there is a gang who is never in school. Ginna is one of them. Worrying about him is like a constant headache – it eats away at my concentration. I have become irritable with Adam and my work has deteriorated. The way things are going, Adam will chuck me and I will fail all my exams.

As usual, I say a little prayer as I make my way home. 'Please God, let Pa have had a good day.' I have said this prayer since Ginna and I were at primary school and Pa first stopped going out. It's got so I can't go home without saying the prayer. I fear that if I ever forget it, something bad might happen. There might be an ambulance waiting outside the house. Or a police car. Men in white coats – men in blue caps – something dreadful. Now I add an extra prayer: 'Please God make Ginna come home and let everything be all right.'

As I walk I wonder what kind of day Pa's had, because Pa's day determines our evening. And you can never judge, or even make a guess, because you can go out in the morning and he's fine (well, as fine as Pa ever is) and then when you get back – chaos.

It's chaos. I might have known. There are six mugs cluttering up the sink and some half-eaten baked beans on a plate on the table. Burnt toast is still under the grill and the house smells. It stinks of burnt food, cigarette smoke and pain. I creep across the cracked black and white floor tiles in the kitchen, hoping against hope that the house is empty. Maybe Pa has gone down to the allotment, is there now doing some digging on this beautiful spring day, spreading compost and humming softly to himself.

But even as these ideas flit across my mind, I know only too well that it has not happened. Pa has not been down to the allotment for over a year. And the memories of him going there are fading, and joining older memories of him waiting outside the school gates for Ginna and me when we were little, or of him getting ready to go out in the evening to do a gig, his guitar case slung over his shoulder.

The sitting-room curtains are pulled against the sunshine and the room is thick with cigarette smoke and sickly sweet joss-sticks. Pa is lying on the settee with an old patchwork quilt over his legs, and I tiptoe across in case he is asleep. His eyes are closed; the pallor of his face merges into the grey straggles of his beard and the pepper and salt of his hair, so I don't feel as if I can see him at all. It's like he's disappearing in front of me.

'Pa?' I whisper. His eyes shoot open, sudden patches of blue amongst all that paleness.

'Fawn, Fawn...' He says my name like an incantation. 'Where's River? You didn't come home alone, did you?'

'Oh no. We got sent home early and I came back in a crowd. Gin— River won't be long. He had some studying to do and was in the library when I left.' I lie cheerfully, telling Pa what he wants to hear, like a mother pacifying an irritable toddler. It works, and he leans back against the merry patchwork pillow with a contented sigh.

'You had a bad day?' I ask consolingly. He nods. 'I'll make you a nice cup of tea. Have you seen the sunshine?' Moving across to the window I tentatively part the curtains a little and open one of the small windows. The smoke from the room coils out into the clean air like blue feathers.

'Tell River to come and see me when he gets home...' Pa says, and I nod as I make my way back into the kitchen. Pa is the only person in the world who calls Ginna by his proper name. I mean, what lad wants to be lumbered with a name like River McKenzie?

After opening the kitchen door to get rid of the stench in the house, I begin to clear the table. Ma works until seven o'clock and so I will have to cook something for tea. Ginna is meant to take turns, but if I force him he goes into the M&S food hall in town and nicks ready-cooked meals: vegetarian stuff for Pa and chicken pies for the rest of us. They are unbelievably good, but I live in terror of Ginna being caught pinching. I don't know what would happen to Pa.

When the kettle is boiling I search for the hidden stash of washing-up liquid Ma keeps out of sight at the back of the cupboard. Pa doesn't like us using anything which harms the environment – we're meant to wash everything with hot water and Sunlight soap. Big deal. As I scrape the beans off the plate I wonder bitterly why Pa is so concerned about the environment, which is a world he has quite literally turned his back on, and yet doesn't mind his own small space on this planet being full of dog-ends and empty tea mugs.

We're on the six o'clock news! It is really weird to see the school and old Bluebottle there on the screen. The school looks awful – all black turrets and high windows, like Count Dracula's castle. And Bluebottle is wearing too much eyeliner and could easily pass for one of the undead. I study her face. She was quite young and pretty when she first came to Meadowlea. Now there are big bags under her eyes and she has developed a nervous tic in one eyelid. I suppose it's a kind of modern-day shell-shock. She is announcing her resignation, citing ill-health. Poor old Bluebottle. When we were under siege from the inspectors she introduced me to a group of them: 'This is Fawn McKenzie, Head Girl and one of our gifted pupils.' Head Girl – that was a laugh. It was just one of poor old Bluebottle's ideas to make us into a posh school. And the harder she tried, the worse it got.

Pa is very upset about the school being on the news. 'What's going on at that school?' he asks in a querulous voice.

'It was just a bad crowd – a few trouble-makers. But most of them have left now…' As I say this, I find myself wishing very hard that Dean Spiers – Spider – had left Meadowlea and was a million miles away from us. Ginna is gulping down his lentil stew, and he gives me a funny look as if he knows what I am thinking. It's strange being a twin – sometimes you do know.

After tea, Pa goes back to the settee and his astrology books and I begin to clear the table.

'Don't dash off!' I say, as Ginna makes for the door still pushing bread into his mouth. 'Pa didn't get up today – the animals need feeding.'

'Oh, come on, Fawn,' he wheedles. 'I've got to go. I'm seeing a man about a dog...' He grins at me, a winning lop-sided smile. 'Just for tonight – please?'

'Just for *every* night,' I grumble. Ginna making the joke about a dog reminds me of when we were young and we still had Merlin, our dog. Ginna didn't go off playing with the bad lads then. We used to come home from school and take Merlin up to the woods, walking miles, even if it was raining. The only reason Pa allowed us to have a dog was if we promised to do that. If Pa has a good day, he goes into the back garden and looks after the animals, but I know he won't have done it today.

I leave Ma's dinner under a plate on top of a saucepan full of hot water and race down to the shed. I have put the immersion on and I want to have a bath and wash my hair before I meet Adam.

The animals all belong to Ginna. He used to breed rabbits, guinea pigs and hamsters, and sell them to the pet shops in town. The bottom of the garden is a testament to his enthusiasm. There are runs and activity courses for the smaller animals, and a bunny compound with pipes and hollowed-out logs so the rabbits can pretend they are in a warren.

Today all the animals have been left in their cages and hutches. For some reason that makes me feel very sad, almost like crying. I don't understand this. I could weep because my school is on the news – one reporter called it a *Lord of the Flies* situation, for heavens' sake! Or I could cry because my twin is turning into a stranger. Instead I am grizzling because the rabbits haven't been let out. I think it's because it's been sunny all day; a rare day when the sky is a high blue dome and the air full of the scent of newness. It seems so wrong that today, of all days, they should have been shut in. One of Pa's dictums in life is that everything is part of God's creation and should be free. And this philosophy is so ingrained in me that I find myself taking the animals out of the hutches and putting them in their runs. Then I fill up the water bowls and feed dishes and watch the animals for a moment, savouring a little warm glow that comes from doing the right thing.

I don't have a warm glow when I realise that Pa has been up to the bathroom and turned the immersion heater off. I wash my hair in luke-warm and then cold water, and say every bad word I can think of as the water glugs away down the plug hole.

Ma is in the kitchen, eating her tea, when I go down. She is much younger than Pa, too young really to be our mother. Her hair is a very pretty gingery red and her eyes are large and brown. When she's dressed up to go out she looks really great, but today she is wearing a very bobbled green jumper over faded black leggings and her hair needs washing.

'He turned the immersion off!' I hiss, and she gives me a sympathetic smile.

'You look nice anyway, Fawn. Oh and thanks for the supper, it's lovely.' It isn't lovely at all. It's lentil, potato and carrot all cooked up together in a pan. But Ma very rarely grumbles.

'Are you and Ginna both out again?' she asks. 'You're never at home these days.' There is a note of regret in her voice which I ignore. My need for Adam is like a pain gnawing at my insides. There is nothing in the world which can keep me from him.

'I won't be late,' I say automatically. Leaving the house is a relief, like being let out of prison. If only Ginna wasn't out with Spider I could almost feel happy.

Adam is waiting for me at the arcade of shops. Some of the little kids are sitting in a doorway playing jacks and the older kids are rollerblading. There is no sign of Ginna and Spider. They think they are too big now to hang around the arcade. Instead they go into town and hang around the bus station, pretending they really are going somewhere. It's pathetic.

Adam and I link hands and walk up to the top of the estate. Because I am so pleased to see him I don't notice for a moment how strange he looks – strung out – as if he's taken something which has made the blood run too quickly through his veins.

We are walking back to his house. He says his mum and step-dad, whom I am allowed to call Barbara and Darren, are having a barbecue and are expecting us. Adam lives at the nicest end of the estate, on top of the hill, where the roads are named after famous poets. Adam lives at Wordsworth Avenue, which I think is really lovely. Down at our end the roads are named after trees.

Before we get there he suddenly stops and pulls me into a space between two garages. The road is very quiet and I feel as if I can hear my heart beating as he kisses me gently. 'Fawn, I'm sorry. There's something I've got to tell you before we get home.'

Suddenly my mouth is dry as a bone, and I swallow hard, feeling that I might choke on the fear which is rising in my throat. 'You're chucking me?' I croak.

'No!' He is too vehement. I know it's bad news, I can see the message in his eyes now – a look laden with sadness, pity and betrayal. I have seen exactly that expression before. It was how Ma looked when we took Merlin to the vet to have him put to sleep. I pull out of Adam's arms as he blurts out: 'We're moving. Mam went mad when she saw the school on the news. She's been dead upset since it was in the paper, but now this. It made her decide. We're taking a Barrett exchange on the house. We're moving next week. They went and signed up this evening. It's all arranged.'

'So quick?' I say, not really believing him.

'They want me to start a new school after the holiday.'

'New school?'

'We're moving out to Boldersby – I'll be going to Briers Park.'

'Not to the sixth-form college?'

We'd talked and made such plans about leaving Meadowlea and going to college together. I can't believe it isn't going to happen.

Adam looks ashamed of his own good fortune as he mumbles: 'Briers Park has a really good sixth form. I won't need to move. It's one reason Mam and Darren chose it. The house is really too expensive. Mam says she'll have to get a job.'

I can't imagine Adam's mum going out to work. Skating out through the front door pulling a brush through her hair, the way Ma does, with the porridge pot still soaking in the sink and the beds unmade.

'Come on, it doesn't have to change things between us, honest,' Adam says. He is frowning at me in a concerned manner. Maybe he thinks I'm going to cry. But I'm like those people in a war whose legs get blown off and they can still feel them. I know this is the end of everything, but it hasn't sunk in yet.

We walk on in silence. My mind is a blank. Part of me is trying to store up memories of this evening. I want to get hold of Adam with his lovely skin and kind blue eyes and keep him forever in my brain. But I realise that if I am to have any chance of staying part of Adam's new life then I must handle this news carefully. 'I'm really pleased for you.' I squeeze his arm. 'It'll be great living out at Boldersby.'

'You can come and stay. We've a spare room. Mam said it would be OK.'

'Yeah...' I grin. 'Great.'

Adam's house is the neatest in the whole road, with lavish ruffled curtains and an immaculate garden. The sight of the house makes my eyes prickle. I can't believe I'll not be seeing it again after next week.

Barbara and Darren are barbecuing in the back garden, but as the evening is cooling down we eat in the kitchen, with the patio doors open to show the night sky. There is a crescent moon so small and frail it looks like half a silver ring that has been thrown into the sky.

Barbara avoids looking at me as she says: 'You've heard about our move?' I nod. 'It's such a shame, this used to be such a nice estate,' she adds, and I nod again. They talk amongst themselves – details about packing and furniture. I don't say anything, but then that's pretty normal. I have never talked much at Adam's house. I just sit and soak up the atmosphere.

It hits me, as I am eating the strawberry cheesecake we have for pud, how much I am going to miss coming here. Once, in English, we read a poem with a line "balm for the soul" – that's the only bit I can remember. But suddenly those words come back to me and I know just what the writer meant. This house has been balm for my soul and I hadn't known it.

Suddenly I have the soppiest idea that I could write a poem about Adam's house. About how every sense tells you this is a haven of cleanliness and normality. A safe place. You can smell it's clean and everything looks new and untouched. It's like a house on the telly adverts – perfect in every way.

'This is such a lovely house. Whoever gets to live here will be really lucky,' I say to Barbara.

'Oh, I don't know,' she says, but her cheeks are pink with pleasure. 'I've done my best. But you wait until you see our new house. I'm going to treat myself and have fresh curtains. Would you like to see the patterns I've chosen?' We go into the dining room and the samples are spread over the glass-topped dining table like a display in a shop.

After a while Adam and I go into the sitting room and watch a film on TV. Because we are alone we snuggle on the settee and kiss a bit. If I shut my eyes very tightly I can almost believe that none of it is true. That we will go back to how things used to be.

At ten o'clock Barbara taps on the door and we know our evening is over. Adam walks me home. He talks about packing up his room and how busy he's going to be. So we arrange to go to the cinema the following Wednesday. It's four days away. We've never gone longer than a day without seeing each other before, except when he's been away on holiday and then he wrote to me every day.

My emotions are so raw when I walk into the hall at home that I hurt with a physical pain. And I know then why songwriters and poets talk about hearts breaking. I look down at the bare boards of the floor, the grubby Indian rugs and the posters on the wall. Suddenly I am so angry I want to shout and scream and rip the posters down and tear them into a million tiny little pieces. I blunder into the kitchen to find it empty. Ma has washed up and wiped the table. She has done her best, and despite my need for revenge I am glad that she has gone to bed.

Then into the stillness of the night comes the unearthly sound of a vixen calling her cubs. The urban foxes don't normally bother us much. There's nothing worth picking over in our dustbin. But the rabbits are out there and the little guinea pigs. Tiredness hits me like a wave. I want to go to bed and curl up with my pain. But the fox screams again, and it sounds nearer. I hear someone in the distance shout: 'Bugger off, blasted nuisance...' and the sound of a missile landing.

From under the sink I find the torch and stumble down to the bottom of the garden. I see the vixen, under the lilac bush. Her coat is rough and there are bald patches on her side. In the trembling beam of light, her eyes glow yellow and malevolent before she moves away into the shadows.

The closeness of the fox has disorientated the little animals and they seem to want to stay out in the dangerous darkness. It takes me ages to catch them all, and by the time I finish I am shivering with cold. The night suddenly seems full of terrors and I wonder when Ginna will be back. Knowing he is out there somewhere in the blackness makes me feel weak.

When I get back into the kitchen Ginna is sitting slumped at the kitchen table. Relief at the sight of him makes me explode into a whispered tirade of abuse.

'Shut up, Fawn...' he says, shaking his head as if I am an irritation.

I grab his hair and pull his head back. His eyes are unfocused and there is a big bruise on the side of his face. The smell of alcohol hangs on his breath.

'You're pissed! And what happened to your face?' I asked, angry with him and enraged that someone has hurt him, all at the same time. Releasing him I whisper: 'What's the matter with you, Ginna? Can't you see what you are doing? Don't you realise what will happen if you go on running around with Spider and the rest of those dead-end kids? You will get nicked! And have you thought what will happen to Pa if the police arrive here and do a search?' His eyes have glazed while I have been talking and I poke his shoulder to make him listen to me. 'Big policemen in big boots, going over the house, looking everywhere. Looking in the cupboards,' I add menacingly.

'It's medicinal! He takes it for pain relief...' Ginna says in defiance.

'Don't be so stupid,' I hiss, my face only inches from his. 'Can you see the magistrates swallowing that one? Grow up. If you want to act bad, wait until you've left home.' My face is right up next to his now. I am cross-eyed with fury. 'And in future put your own rabbits in,' I add, pushing him suddenly away from me.

The tears don't start until I'm in bed and curled like an unborn child beneath the bedclothes. Only then do I face the fact that I'm angry with the whole world: with Adam, Ma and Pa, Spider, Bluebottle, with the journalists who invaded our school today and especially with Ginna.

I couldn't feel more lonely and bereft if I had been abandoned on an inhospitable island. The whole fabric of my life seems to have moved and shifted, leaving me completely isolated. Meadowlea has always been a hard school, but now it's like a battlefield. Ginna has grown so far away from me it's as if I don't know him any more. And now Adam has deserted me. I know it isn't his fault he is moving, but I feel it like a betrayal. I have lost Adam and my twin and there is no one in the world to comfort me.

2

Once Adam moves away, being with him is like watching someone drowning in slow-motion. The tide of his new life seems to draw him further and further away from me. At times it's as if he is disappearing completely under the waves and I am filled with total panic. Then he bobs back, and, for a moment, I catch a glimpse of what there was between us. But then, slowly and painfully, he is swept away again.

It reminds me of when Merlin was sick and we watched him get thinner and thinner. His appetite diminished until he couldn't eat dog or cat food and Ma fed him baby food for a few days. Then all he could manage was water, great bowls full that he would lap and guzzle as if he'd been lost in a desert. 'It's his kidneys,' Ma said knowledgeably; she had been training to be a nurse when she met Pa and got pregnant with us, so she knows about these things. 'We'll take him to the vet,' she'd added. And because I was just a little kid I thought the vet would make him better. It was when I caught a glimpse of Ma's face as we walked into the surgery that the inevitability of Merlin's death struck me full in the stomach. I hated her for a moment until I saw the tears coursing down her cheeks too.

Now there is the same slow march towards death when I am with Adam. He tries to get me interested in Boldersby, talks of the sports centre where we can go swimming, tells me stories about the gang of kids who hang around outside the chippy. He even announces that Barbara is decorating their spare room in my favourite colours. But, like poor Merlin, my hold on this life is getting weaker and I can summon no interest in any of these things.

'Ring me Thursday,' Adam suggests, as he kisses me tenderly. He is very gentle and kind to me these days, and Barbara and Darren keep on asking me how I am, as if I have some awful incurable illness. For some reason this irks me and I hate the idea of the three of them talking about 'poor Fawn'.

So I don't phone on Thursday, just to be contrary. I leave it until Friday. I think I have some loopy idea that this will make Adam jealous and he will assume that my life is so full and busy I've forgotten to ring him. But when I ring on Friday there is an embarrassed pause, and then Barbara says: 'I'm sorry, Fawn, he's out.'

'That's OK. I'll phone soon...' The pips go, my money has run out. I push open the door of the booth and walk stiff-faced past an old lady who is waiting for the phone. My head feels as if it will explode from all the tears waiting to fall.

It is all over between us. I have known it for weeks now. And, finally, all the feelings which I have been suppressing come rushing into my mind. I look down at my trembling hands. I have lost Adam and the pain is making me feel crazy. And for the first time in my life, when something really dreadful has happened, there is no Ginna to turn to.

When I was a little girl I used to look forward to growing up. I look at the young kids making sand pies in a pile of gravel, the summer evening full of their laughter, and for a moment I envy them.

Adam and I have been going out since I was thirteen – when I was a child with a woman's body. Now, with anger, I realise I have wasted a great big chunk of my life on him. Once we started dating I had no time for any other close friends, so now he has abandoned me I have no one.

Dull-eyed I walk into the house. The kitchen is full of steam. Ma is at the sink washing clothes. 'I've got your overall ready for the morning,' she says. I've got a holiday job working in a supermarket, on the cash-till. It is mind-numbingly boring but I like earning money. Ma hobbles across the kitchen and reaches into the cupboard, wincing with pain.

'What have you done?' I ask, roused out of my self-pity by her obvious agony.

'I've twisted my ankle. It'll be all right. I've strapped it up. I'll have to be all right for tomorrow. Mrs Charles has asked me to work all day. She's giving a lunch party and the children are at home.' Ma says this with a grimace, as if the children being at home is the equivalent to having wild tigers in the house.

'Well, can't they help her?' I ask with sudden aggression.

'Oh dear no! They can't lift a finger to do anything,' Ma says irritably. 'I dread the holidays. You should see it there – clothes everywhere, and the state of the bathrooms! It takes me hours to clear up after them, and Mrs Charles still expects the silver cleaned and the windows to be sparkling.'

'Well, you can't go if you're not well,' I say, angry and jealous at the idea of Ma having to clean up after the Charles' children.

'I've got to. She's paying me time and a half and this is my under-the-counter job. I get cash in hand, no questions...' Ma adds, as if I'm thick or something.

'I'll go for you. You can phone the shop and say I'm ill. They'll have all the Saturday kids in so it'll be all right.'

'Bless you, darling,' Ma says, as she hugs me. And I think to myself that this is the beginning of my life without Adam and I feel so miserable I don't care what happens to me.

I begin to care when I realise I have to ride Ma's bike to get to this job. Even on our estate there are standards. To be seen on Ma's bike is the equivalent of social death. 'I'll walk,' I say stubbornly. 'I'm not riding all the way along the Harrogate Road on that heap of rusting metal!'

'Oh, I'll go myself,' Ma cries out in temper. 'It'll take you hours to walk it. And you'll be exhausted by the time you get there.'

'All right,' I say grudgingly. Ma has made me wear my smartest black school skirt and a white top because, she says, 'Mrs Charles is very fussy, especially when there are visitors in the house.'

I have already decided that I don't like the sound of Mrs Charles. And she doesn't rise in my estimation as I walk through the estate, head held high, pretending I'm simply taking this ghastly old bike to the shop to have a puncture repaired. Once on the main road I'm so tired I'm grateful to get on the bike and coast along.

The Charles' house knocks me out. Ma told me it was beautiful, but I am unprepared for the long sweep of green lawns, the immaculate flower beds and huge trees. The house is made from soft grey stone with mullion windows twinkling and winking in the sunlight. I freewheel up the long drive, gazing in admiration, until I realise people may be looking out from the windows. I jump off quickly and sling the bike into the laurel bushes. There are steps leading up to the front door and an ornate metal bell pull. I am so enraptured with it all that I grab the handle and clang the door bell. The heavy tolling which echoes through the house brings me to my senses.

'I'm so sorry,' I stutter, red-faced, as the door opens. 'I think I should have gone around to the back door.'

'It's OK,' an amused voice answers. 'You won't be shot at

dawn, at least not until after the lunch party. You must be Fawn... Freaky! I've never seen anyone who actually looks like their name.'

Looking across at the speaker I am horribly embarrassed. Firstly by his posh voice – there isn't a trace of Yorkshire in it – and secondly by the fact that he is a tall, lean, young male wearing shorts and a vivid multicoloured T-shirt which tells the world he holidays in the USA.

'I'm Fawn McKenzie,' I say, which is incredibly stupid because he already knows my name. But he just grins and says:

'Come on down to the kitchen and have a drink. You look hot.'

'I'm here to work,' I say a bit abruptly, to hide my confusion. I would guess that the boy is my age or a little older. He has black hair, swept back from his face, and eyes so dark they look nearly black. His face is long and bony, not good-looking, or handsome like Adam, but clear-skinned and intelligent.

'The dogs are in the kitchen. Do you want me to shut them in the utility room?' he says over his shoulder, as he leads me down the hall and through a door which leads to the back of the house.

'Oh no, I love dogs.'

'You may not love these two,' he warns ominously.

In the kitchen the Bull Mastiffs mob me. They are the size of young donkeys with velvet coats and black eyes. I kneel on the floor and let them sniff me. Then I run my hands over their solid nut-brown shoulders. When we are friends I put my arms around their necks and let them lick my chin and cheeks. They nuzzle and kiss me and whispered baby-words of endearment rise to my lips.

'You aren't joking! You do love dogs,' the boy says, laughing as he takes a can of Coke from an enormous fridge and opens it for me. 'For the first time in my life I wish I was a dog,' he adds cryptically. And I rise to my feet, feeling foolish, but strangely happy. 'Here you are, Fawn McKenzie,' he adds, handing the Coke to me.

'Thanks.' I wipe dog slobber from my chin with the back of my hand. 'They're lovely dogs. I wish my brother could see them, he's crazy about dogs,' I add, and the boy grins at me without speaking.

I am saved from any more idiotic remarks by the arrival of Mrs Charles. She looks like her son, who I find is called Simon. Her hair too is swept straight back from her face but the blackness is contrasted by a sharp silver streak in the front. Her eyes are wrinkly but kind.

'Fawn, my dear,' she says enthusiastically. 'How good of you to come and help us. How is your mother's ankle? Now, where did you leave your bicycle?'

My face heats again. 'In the bushes,' I mutter. There is a little sprinkle of laughter between the boy and his mother from which I am excluded.

'Simon, go and fetch the bicycle and leave it by the back door. Fawn will need it to get home later. Come along Fawn, we'll start with the bathrooms.'

Mrs Charles puts on a PVC pinny and hands me another. This is obviously serious cleaning. She takes me upstairs and into the main bedroom, which is decorated in pink and gold with a four-poster bed. It looks like a film set. In the centre of the room there is a trolley waiting for me, piled up with clean towels and cleaning materials.

'This is my bedroom,' she says with a smile. 'So it's nice and tidy. There's just the bed to make. I'm afraid you won't find Simon and Esther's rooms so easy. Now first – the bathroom.' She marches in a determined fashion into the en suite. The basin and bath are emerald green with gold taps.

My mouth falls open with admiration. 'Gosh! It's beautiful!' I blurt out. Mrs Charles smiles at me sympathetically. I wonder what is happening in my astrological chart for today, because I am giving a good imitation of being half-witted.

'Now, Fawn.' Mrs Charles has donned rubber gloves. 'This is how I like the toilet and bath cleaned.' By the time she has finished my head is whirling with colour-coded cloths and different sprays. 'Do you think you can manage that?' I nod. 'Now for the beds...' she adds. I shake and smooth the bed into shape and she nods with approval. 'Good girl, you can do the other bedrooms and bathrooms and then come down to the kitchen for a coffee.'

My euphoria with silk sheets and the trolley evaporates when I walk into Simon's room. It looks like it has been vandalised. Drawers have been pulled out, the contents ransacked and then left. There is a trail of clothes and damp towels leading to the bathroom. The window is shut and the room smells.

Opening the windows wide I begin to pick up crumpled clothes and wet towels and jam them into the bin-bag hanging from the trolley.

'Sorry about the mess.' Simon is leaning on the door frame, watching me as I gingerly pick up a pair of socks and then shove them hastily into the washing bag.

'That's all right. It's what I'm paid to do. Not that I'd want someone sorting out my washing and bed-clothes.' Ripping back the duvet I begin to straighten the sheet.

'What do you mean by that?' He doesn't sound annoyed, more curious.

'Well, it's like you're an invalid or disabled or something. I mean, grown-up people shouldn't need their clothes picked up for them, should they?'

I say this very innocently. In fact it makes me sick to think that he leaves his sweaty socks on the floor for my mother to collect. I realise he is staring at me very hard and wonder if I have gone too far. I begin to quickly straighten out the contents of the drawers and shut them. Outside there are the sounds of summer: the whirr of a lawn mower and bird song, streaming in through the window along with the sunshine.

'It's lovely to hear the birds singing, isn't it?' I say, as I cast a glance around the now tidy room and make my way over to the bathroom. He follows me and stands in the doorway, watching me again.

'Don't you have birds where you live?'

'Not ones which sing. Only pigeons and starlings.' I busy myself with cleaning the toilet. When I look up he has gone.

Esther's room is marginally better than Simon's. More clothes, but they don't stink and the bathroom isn't swimming with water. I finish pretty quickly. Esther's room is my favourite so far – it has climbing roses on the wallpaper, a sugar-pink carpet and white lace curtains. Classy!

When I finally finish and go down to the kitchen I find Simon waiting. There is instant coffee ready in a mug and a big piece of creamy cake sitting on a plate. 'Sit down, Fawn,' he says, pulling out a chair for me.

'Thanks,' I say. The sight of the cake is making my mouth water. That bike ride has given me an appetite. Breakfast at home seems part of another lifetime.

'The cake's for you,' he adds, as if reading my mind.

'Thanks,' I say again, and tuck in. I have just finished when Mrs Charles pops her head around the door.

'Oh, is Simon looking after you?' she says with surprise. 'I thought Esther was making coffee.'

'She's on the phone,' Simon says. He sits down opposite me and stares. 'Would you like another piece of cake?' he asks at last.

Realising I have eaten the cake far too quickly for good manners I shake my head and stir my coffee. 'No thanks, that was lovely.'

'Go on, have another little bit. Mum makes wonderful cakes.'

He reaches into the fridge and is just putting another slice of cake on my plate when Mrs Charles comes back into the kitchen. She says crossly: 'Simon, what on earth do you think you're doing? That coffee gâteau is for lunch.'

Looking guiltily down at my plate I mumble: 'Sorry.' Suddenly the sickly coffee flavour and the rich cream of the icing has made me feel sick.

'Sorry, does it matter?' Simon says, and he doesn't sound at all sorry. 'I just thought Fawn might like a piece.'

'I'm sure Fawn would, but in future we'll stick to biscuits in the middle of the morning, shall we?' Mrs Charles's tone is very frosty – rather like a cross headmistress. I rise to my feet, my face feels like a beetroot.

'I'm ever so sorry,' I say, looking down at the slice of cake and cup of coffee on the table. 'I wouldn't have had any if I'd known...'

'Well, it isn't your fault, Fawn,' Mrs Charles says, although she is plainly annoyed. 'I shall have to get a Black Forest gâteau out of the freezer and hope it defrosts in time.'

'Chill out, Mum. There's heaps of stuff for lunch,' Simon says casually. 'What does it matter if a slice of cake is missing? No one will notice.'

He walks out of the room. I wish I could walk out too and get away from Mrs Charles's beady black-eyed stare. She is eyeing me as if seeing me for the first time. I nervously wipe the corners of my mouth with my thumb, wishing I had a hanky.

'Sorry,' I say lamely, and then more brightly: 'What would you like me to do next? I've finished the bedrooms.'

'You can dust and vacuum the downstairs rooms,' she says, and bustles me out of the kitchen. My cup of coffee, which is untouched, and the second piece of cake, are left abandoned. I feel her reproach like a heat on my skin as she shows me where the dusters and the vacuum are kept.

While I am dusting the silver on the sideboard next to the service hatch I hear Mrs Charles say dismissively: 'Oh, she's pretty enough, but that skirt is too short.'

There is laughter and I hear Simon say: 'Lovely, but intellectually challenged!'

Suddenly self-conscious, I pull my skirt down and blink away the tears of temper and hurt which have risen in my eyes. I wish I could walk into the kitchen and tell Mrs Charles to stick her job. And then tell her slobby children to pick up their own dirty socks. I'd like to say and do a lot of things but I know that Ma really needs this particular job. Cash in hand. It means a lot.

The hatch swings open. 'Fawn! What are you doing there?'

There are three surprised faces looking at me. Mrs Charles looks uncomfortable, as if she suspects I might have overheard their conversation. Esther is smiling at me. She is just like her brother, only her hair is long and hangs at the sides of her bony face like two straight black curtains.

'I'm dusting,' I say defiantly. 'Just like you told me to.'

'I thought I *asked* you to please start in the drawing room,' Mrs Charles says with calm deliberation.

Looking around the room with its long table and mirror-topped sideboard, I mutter miserably: 'I thought this was... I mean...'

Mrs Charles and Esther exchange looks. 'Well, never mind,' Mrs Charles says. 'Carry on in there. You're doing a marvellous job, Fawn,' she adds. 'Esther was just saying how lovely her room looks.'

'Yes,' Esther says, smiling at me. 'Thank you, Fawn.'

Staring back at them, my face and mind are blank with rage. I say mutinously: 'I'm not waiting at table during lunch.'

'But your mother always does,' Mrs Charles says soothingly. 'And you've worn your nice skirt and blouse so you really look the part.'

'Yes, well, I don't want to do it now. I might drop something.' I refuse to look at them as I twist the duster around in my fingers.

'It's all right, Mummy,' Esther says quickly. 'Simon and I will hand things round and put everything through the hatch. Don't make Fawn do it if she doesn't want to.'

The note of genuine sympathy in her voice makes my eyes fill and I turn and begin to polish the table as if demented. Behind me I hear the hatch being closed.

I work until I feel that I might drop to the floor with weariness. During the lunch party I wash up in the kitchen listening to the voices coming through the hatch. There is lots of laughter. At two o'clock, when they are all having pudding, Mrs Charles gives me a plate of cold meat and salad.

'Sit down for twenty minutes, make yourself a cup of tea if you like,' she says. There is a pause, when I know she is waiting for me to say thank you, but I can't. 'Not much longer now,' she adds, with a tight smile. I get the feeling she will be pleased to see the back of me.

As this is my lunch break I let the dogs, Troy and Casper, out from the utility room and share the meat on my plate with them. They take it with surprising gentleness from my fingers and then stretch out under the table and watch me with adoring eyes. I touch them with my foot as I finish the salad and talk nonsense to them. Then I make a pot of tea and find the digestive biscuits. Casper, Troy and I have two each.

'I've brought you a piece of Black Forest gâteau,' says a voice. It is Simon, smiling and looking very pleased with himself. 'I swiped it before they could guzzle the lot.' He looks down at the piece of cake with satisfaction.

'I don't want it,' I snap, biting my lip to stop myself from saying more. 'I don't like cake,' I add waspishly, and he retreats, looking puzzled.

At four o'clock I finally finish washing up and clearing the kitchen. 'You've been a great help,' Mrs Charles says, pressing bank-notes into my hand. There is five pounds more than Ma is usually paid. 'I've paid you some extra, as you were so kind to come at short notice,' she adds, with a smile that does not reach her eyes.

The money should cheer me up, but it doesn't, because I am too tired and dispirited to care about anything. I feel as if I could go to sleep on my feet. This is the hardest I have ever worked in my entire life. And I marvel at Ma's stamina because during the week she goes from here to an evening cleaning job. Pocketing the money, I leave without a word.

Outside, the afternoon is sunny and sweet-smelling. I find the bike balancing against the kitchen wall, and knowing that Simon has retrieved it and placed it there for me makes me feel doubly humiliated.

As I push the bike down the drive I hear the sound of an engine. I look steadfastly ahead as I am overtaken by a red jeep. It pulls up outside the gates and Simon jumps down. 'Want a lift?' he asks, grinning.

'I've got a bike,' I say sulkily, looking away.

'Oh, come on, Fawn. I'll put it in the back and drive you home. You've got a puncture anyway.' Looking down I see that he is right. The back tyre is completely flat. The Harrogate Road stretches before me and my legs seem to buckle at the thought of the long walk.

'Come on,' he says with a touch of impatience, taking hold of the bike handles. 'I don't see what all the fuss is about. Get in.'

Reluctantly I slide into the seat next to him and pull my skirt down. We drive in silence. The journey takes only a matter of minutes in a car. When we get to the top of the estate I say quickly: 'Just drop me here, I'll walk the rest.'

'Don't you want me to see where you live?' His eyes are very black and piercing, suddenly unfriendly.

'I don't care,' I mutter. 'Everywhere is grotty around here. Just some bits are worse than others. It's left here, down to the bottom of the hill and then third on the right. Elm Road. Number twenty.'

He negotiates the narrow roads carefully, frowning still. As he parks outside our house he looks around at the shabby red-brick houses and untidy gardens – but his gaze is inscrutable. 'Bit different to where you live, isn't it?' I say stiffly, reaching for the door. 'Thanks for the lift, anyway.'

'Fawn, wait!'

'I'll get my bike out,' I say ungraciously, ignoring him.

'Fawn!' He says my name so urgently that I turn back to face him. He swallows, bites his bottom lip and blurts out: 'Would you like to go out to the cinema tonight?' I suspect he is nervous; he is unable to meet my eyes and fidgets with the steering wheel while he waits for my answer.

'I don't think so...' I say coolly.

'Why not?' He sneaks a glance at me. Now I know he's nervous; it's written in his eyes.

'Because I'm the cleaner and intellectually challenged into the bargain...' I say very deliberately, and he winces.

'I'm sorry,' he says. 'I was just shooting my mouth off. I don't think you're stupid at all. I just didn't want my mother and Esther to...'

'Know that you were going to ask me out?' I finish crisply for him. 'So what will you tell them this evening?'

'You will come then?' He looks so thrilled and happy that it is my turn to wince. I have never liked to hurt dumb animals.

'No. I won't,' I say firmly.

'Please Fawn, just give me a chance to make up for – well – you know.'

Just as I am about to say 'No' again I see Pa's face at the window peeping through a gap in the curtains. My spirits sudden sag. Tonight there will be no Adam and an evening at home stretches ahead of me – hours of utter cheerlessness. There is no chance that Ginna will stay in. I will be stuck with Pa playing records and Ma knitting. The thought makes me want to scream. I weigh up the two options: going out with Simon or staying in.

'OK, what time?' I say without enthusiasm. You would think I was being taken to the dentist.

He looks astonished that I have suddenly agreed, but very pleased. There is something about the delight in his eyes which makes me feel a bit sick, as if I have just eaten another slice of the coffee gâteau. 'I'll pick you up here at about six-thirty. We can have something to eat. But not cake!' he adds with a grin.

As I walk up the broken concrete of our front path and hear his jeep roar off up the road I am filled with desolation. When I get to the side of the house I lean for a moment against the wall. Tiredness seems to have seeped into every part of me, so that I am weary in mind and spirit as well as in body.

If only I could turn the clock back to when Meadowlea was just another inner-city school and not headline news; to a time when Adam was still my boyfriend and best friend; back to when Ginna was my bro and not some slouching stranger with a grudge against the whole world.

Somehow, agreeing to go out with Simon has made it all seem worse instead of better. It has thrown into sharp focus the troubles and loneliness of my life. Because now, as if losing Adam wasn't bad enough, I'm going out with someone whom I don't like and who thinks I'm dim. And I really must be stupid, and desperate, I think savagely, to be going out on a date with Simon Charles!

3

Pa is waiting for me, lurking behind the kitchen door like a ghost, as if the sunshine slicing across the dirty floor might somehow contaminate him. 'Who was that in the car?'

'It was Simon Charles, he gave me a lift. Ma's bike got a puncture. Where is Ma?'

'Her ankle swelled up, she's gone to the hospital. Where's River?' Pa pleads. 'He's been out all day.'

'River's at work,' I say patiently, putting the kettle on the gas and beginning to stack the dirty plates from the table. Pa has been eating toast, wholemeal toast with lots of honey. This is comfort eating – he must be upset.

'I'm sure River didn't go to work, his overall's still hanging on the back of his bedroom door,' Pa explains anxiously.

'Well I don't know, do I?' I'm irritable to hide my fear. 'Maybe he's got a spare overall. Where else would he be?' Ginna has a Saturday job helping at a garage, he's been odd-jobbing there for years. Mr Thomas, the owner, will go mad if he hasn't turned up. I know Ginna doesn't have a spare overall and fear makes my face go clammy and I feel weak inside.

Pa is still standing behind me, fingers twisting in his beard, which is what he does when he is worried. Maybe it is all the fidgeting he does with his beard that has made it so thin and wispy. Desperate to get away from him, I run upstairs to the bathroom and lock myself in. Leaning against the door, I try to control my erratic breathing and fast-beating heart. If Ginna hasn't gone to work he will have no money for the coming week. We buy our own lunches, sweets and clothes from the money we earn. The fiver Mrs Charles has given me won't go far between the two of us. Anger and fear fill me up so I feel like screaming.

There is a rattling on the door: 'Fawn, Fawn, are you all right?' And for one idiotic moment I think I might actually have made a noise.

'I'm fine, Pa. Out in a moment.' I flush the loo and then splash my face with cold water. Then I open the airing cupboard and flick on the hot-water switch. As I leave the bathroom, Pa comes out from his bedroom. 'The water-heater is on,' I say very deliberately. 'Please don't turn it off.'

Pa follows me down the stairs, flip-flopping in his old slippers. 'Cold water is good for the skin, Fawn.'

'I want a bath. I'm going out tonight. And I want to wash my hair.'

'There's some rainwater in the barrel, that's good for hair.

But you shouldn't wash your hair too often, you know, Fawn. It isn't good for it – strips it of the natural oils.' He has followed me into the kitchen.

'I don't want to wash my hair in rainwater,' I say quietly, as I make a pot of tea and then pour the rest of the boiling water into the washing-up bowl.

'Where are you going? I don't like you going out in the evening except with Adam or River.'

I pour him a mug of tea and he sits down at the kitchen table and sips it. 'I'm going out with Simon Charles, the boy who brought me home. I'm sixteen, Pa. I am old enough to go out without a chaperone.' As I begin washing up he talks about a tribe of Indians in South America who clean their hair by smothering it in mud, but I am busy at the sink, only half listening.

Suddenly he says: 'I wish you and River would stay at home more. We used to have such good times. Reading *The Lord of the Rings* in the evenings... Maybe we should read it again...'

His wistful voice fades away and, for a moment, I am taken back to my childhood. When Ginna and I were young, Pa played in a rock band and wore bright shirts and jeans. Sometimes I would wake in the night and hear the group laughing and talking in the kitchen. Then, the next day, we would be told by Ma to keep quiet and would creep around the house in our socks, talking in whispers so he could sleep until noon. I remember Pa when he had dark hair and twinkly eyes, and would drink home-made beer and read to

45

us in the evenings before he went off to work. He started with *The Hobbit* when we were ten years old and Ginna and I were hooked. After that it took him about a year to read us *The Lord of the Rings*... and somehow when the book ended so did the good times. He is talking about it now as if reading aloud to us could weave some kind of spell. I sigh. If only Pa really could solve all our problems.

Pa doesn't give me a chance to tell Ma about Simon Charles. He blurts it out as soon as she comes in through the door. She has a thick bandage on her ankle and is walking with the aid of a metal walking stick.

'It's a bad sprain. But it feels so much better now I've got it strapped up. It will be all right. I'll still be able to work.' Pa goes off to smoke and watch the TV and Ma says: 'What's all this about Simon taking you out? What about Adam?'

'Adam and I are history,' I say bleakly, drying the plates and mugs. 'I thought it would be cool to go out with someone else,' I add with a shrug.

'I don't think it's a good idea, Fawn.' Ma looks really upset. 'Simon is very spoilt – he gets everything he wants at home.'

'So?'

'Well, he is quite a lot older than you.'

'He's only about eighteen.' My voice is icy now.

'Why don't you try to patch it up with Adam...' she suggests softly.

'How can Adam and I have a relationship when he is in Boldersby and I am stuck here?' I hiss at her. I'd like to shout but I don't want Pa to hear and come back into the kitchen. 'He doesn't drive. I don't drive. We're not on the phone.'

'He could cycle,' Ma says with dignity. 'If you both wanted to, you could find a way.'

'Cycle! It's bloody miles! And what are we going to do when he's cycled here? Sit in the front room with Pa and do Tarot readings?'

Ma sighs and I feel really bad that I have taken my frustration out on her.

'Just be careful with Simon, that's all I'm saying. He'll only be after one thing...' she says bluntly.

My face flames. 'What a great opinion you have of me!' I spit out. 'Start a fan club for me, why don't you? Do you think I am such a dumb-head that boys only ask me out to try it on?'

'No, I don't mean that,' Ma says tearfully. 'But I know the kind of boy Simon Charles is... Please don't be offended, Fawn. I only want to warn you. You are my baby. I can't bear the thought of you being hurt.'

'Oh shut up!' I shout and march off upstairs. The water is only luke-warm. But I don't care. I lock myself in the bathroom and wash my hair, thinking miserably that Ma is right. What other reason could a boy like Simon Charles have for asking me out?

The red jeep arrives ten minutes early with a roar of the engine and a squeal of brakes. Net curtains the entire length of Elm Road twitch and lift.

Pa stumbles over to the window. 'Is that boy a safe

driver?' he demands. Ma's eyes are filled with anxiety and I can see she is far more worried about other kinds of safety.

Because I am still smarting from our showdown in the kitchen I reply tersely:

'We're only going into town. It's only a couple of miles and I'll tell him not to be such a pathetic little show-off when he's driving.'

'Why are you going out with him if you don't like him?' Ma asks with a frown.

The words *Because I can't bear to spend an evening here with Pa* spring to my lips but I stop myself just in time. Sometimes in the past I haven't been so tactful, and Ma always goes on about how lucky we are not to come back to an empty house and be latch-key children. I know she would remind me that Pa is kind and interested in us, keen for us to do well, and add, with one of her sad resigned smiles, that some kids have much worse fathers. And I know this to be true. It's just sometimes knowing all that doesn't help. And I don't have the words to describe how difficult I find living with Pa now he never leaves the house. Because he is always here, he seems to fill up all the spaces at home. Like the odour of joss-sticks, he seeps into every corner and crevice of the house so there is no room for the rest of us.

Pa is turning down the record player and saying: 'Before you go Fawn...' He flaps a closely written page from a notebook at me. 'I've been consulting the Ephemeris and these are important times for you. In your chart there is a strong link between your natal Pluto and Venus. Pluto,' he says with a nod, 'the planet that heralded the discovery of plutonium. You must handle these energies carefully.'

Looking at Ma's face, I think she's going to cry. This is just what she doesn't want to hear. 'Thanks Pa, I'll bear that in mind,' I say, as I sidle into the hall. Ma follows me. Pa has turned up the record player and is at the window again. He is peeking out at an impatient-looking Simon, who is now standing at our broken front gate as if undecided whether to come in and get me or not.

'Please be careful, Fawn!' Ma whispers. You'd think Simon was the Devil incarnate come to carry me off to Hell the way she is going on.

My temper rises. 'Look! The last thing in the world I want to be is a school-girl mother,' I whisper furiously. 'I want to get away from this dump and make something of my life. So don't start getting jumpy and neurotic just because I'm going out on a date.'

The hurt on her face cuts into me. 'Pa and I have always done our best to give you and Ginna a happy home,' she says miserably. 'We may not have much money but there has always been a lot of love in this house.'

'Spare me the hippy clap-trap...' I mutter. I know that all my anger about Adam, Ginna and school is being directed at her but now I've started I just can't stop. 'Anyway, you are hardly in a position to hand out good advice. Peace and free love didn't get you very far,' I add bitterly.

This is just about the most hateful thing I could possibly say. And as soon as the words are out I wish I could snatch them back and stifle them. But I have given them life and they echo, dancing like wicked little demons, down the dusty floorboards of the hallway. Ma turns away from me to hide the tears in her eyes.

Rage stops me saying that I am sorry. I tell myself I don't care, but as soon as I am out of the door and it is too late, I care like hell.

'Cheer up. It may never happen.' Simon's eyes light up when he sees me.

'It already has,' I say, ignoring his hand waiting to help me into the jeep.

'Please don't drive too fast,' I add sulkily, as we head off down the dual carriageway towards town. He immediately slows down to about twenty miles an hour and an old man in the car behind toots his horn and overtakes us, shaking his head.

'Does that suit you, madam?' Simon asks, and I nod. 'I have to go back to school on Monday. I wish I didn't.' He gives me a sideways glance. 'Will you come out with me tomorrow? I thought we could go to Ilkley – take the dogs on to the moor.'

'Hang on a minute!' It seems that this evening I must be vile to everyone. 'We haven't got through this evening yet! You may decide you can't bear the sight of me by ten. By the way, I have to be home by ten-thirty – ten-forty-five at the latest.'

'That's very strict.'

'I'm only sixteen,' I say primly. 'And my parents are very fussy.'

'That's OK. Look, Fawn, I know already that I want to see you tomorrow, and the day after that if it were possible.' He is so intense that I am embarrassed. Adam and I started going out together when we were still kids, and he never talked to me like that. It seems very grown up and heavy – especially on a first date.

'Well, you're not going to be here so it hardly matters, does it?' I mutter. He shoots a smile across at me.

'I just want you to know...'

'What's your school like?' I ask, to change the subject.

'It's all boys – absolute hell! I can't wait to leave. I liked it when I was a kid but it's so boring now. Which school do you go to, Fawn?'

This is a moment I have rehearsed in my head and dreaded. 'Meadowlea,' I say quietly. My voice doesn't tremble but I shake inside and bow my head awaiting his reaction.

'MEADOWLEA! The school that's been on the news?' I nod. 'Wow!' he adds. 'That must be a real experience.' Is it my imagination or is there a trace of admiration in his voice?

'Is it really as bad as people say? One of the teachers was sexually assaulted, wasn't she?'

I hate the salacious note in his voice. He is finding questioning me exciting, and he reminds me of the kind of person who slows down to look at car crashes. 'Come on, Fawn,' he encourages me. 'Dish the dirt.'

I don't know why I decide to tell him about it. Maybe

because it's the only advantage that I have over him. I go to the worst school in the country and survive.

'There are quite a few rough kids at the school,' I say slowly. 'And they do play up the teachers who can't cope.'

'And are there many of those?'

'We seem to have had quite a few in recent years.'

'Tell me about the teacher who was raped.'

'She wasn't raped!' I say, shocked. 'She was a bundle of nerves and it all got too much for her. The boys sometimes do stupid things. Dropping pencils on the floor and then trying to look up the girls' skirts. It's real kids' stuff. Well, a couple of the boys did that to her and she freaked out. She fell over and the boys were down on the floor too so it all got very nasty. Then she had a kind of fit and was taken off in an ambulance. It was only a matter of time before something pushed her over the edge.'

'God! How awful!' Simon laughs. 'What did she teach?'

'Music and Drama. We haven't had a music lesson since she left. Bluebottle, the headmistress, expelled quite a few kids and suspended a lot more. It was like a grand clear-out. Anyone who had ever been any bother at all got the old heave-ho. Trouble was, they all got into gangs and started coming into school, wrecking classrooms, starting fires, having fights in the corridors. It got totally out of hand. The problem was that there was nothing else that could be done with them. They'd already been shut out from school. It became like a game to them. And I suppose they were bored.'

'How crazy!'

'It's not crazy for people like me who just want to get an education and a job at the end of it,' I say bitterly. I hate myself suddenly for talking about it to him. I feel like a creep.

We are pulling into the big area of wasteland which has been cleared for parking in the city centre. Immediately my attention is taken up by a gang of boys hanging around at the deserted end of the car park. The huddle they are in, the set of their shoulders and the furtive way they look around tells me they are trouble-makers. What upsets me is that I am sure one of them is Ginna. You always know your twin, even at a distance.

'Would you like Chinese or Italian?' Simon asks, smiling into my eyes.

'What?' My thoughts are still on Ginna.

'To eat?' he says patiently.

'Oh, I don't care.'

'You should say you don't mind,' he corrects me gently. But I am too taken up with my worries to care or mind about what he thinks.

'You choose,' I say distractedly.

'I want you to choose.'

'Look,' I snap. 'I don't mind, I don't care. I don't give a monkey's.' I can see Ginna clearly now and part of me wants to run over and find out where he has been all day and what he has been doing. My eyes are suddenly full of tears. Simon immediately assumes he has upset me and takes hold of my hand.

53

'I'm sorry, we'll have Italian. I just want you to have a good time.'

And so I am led off, like a meek lamb, away from my bro, away from my twin. I know he is in trouble and my heart is breaking.

Anxiety turns me into a zombie. I can't eat the pizza. I can't drink the Coke. Simon insists we have profiteroles and I can't eat those either. After forcing down a few mouthfuls I go to the ladies and try to make myself sick. My mind simply can't believe that I have walked away from Ginna – that I am sitting in a restaurant in my best clothes pretending to be a little lady just to keep Simon happy.

When I get back to the table he is sitting, frowning. His face composes into a smile when he sees me. 'Come on. I've paid the bill. Let's get off to the cinema. Maybe you'll enjoy that.'

He takes hold of my hand and I am too torn up inside to care. In fact it is comforting to have his warm hand holding mine. It brings back echoes of Adam.

There is shouting and noise coming from the city centre square which we have to cross to get to the cinema. Flocks of starlings are trying to come in to roost for the evening. But they are flying in a whirling chaotic cloud. Something has unsettled them. Immediately I am tense.

'What's the matter?' Simon asks.

'There's trouble in the square,' I breathe.

'Oh come on, Fawn. It isn't late. It will just be kids.'

But as we emerge from the underpass into the square I

spot Spider. He has climbed up on to the statue of a famous general on horseback. His cronies are jumping off benches and tubs of flowers. They have up-ended litter bins and there is rubbish everywhere.

In the middle of all of this, lounging on a bench with a can of strong cider in his hand, is my brother. We make eye contact and he has the grace to look away. He is ashamed that I have caught him. But, as if to defy me, he takes a great long swig from the can, and when it is empty he throws it up into the air as high as it will go. It lands in one of the dusty trees imprisoned in a concrete box on the edge of the square. The few starlings which have roosted there fly up in jagged disarray, their chattering cries mixing with the shouts of the boys. The birds move like filings to a magnet, a dusky iridescent shadow tracing a graceful arc into the darkening sky, meeting with the returning flock. And suddenly, as if there is safety in numbers, they all return to the tree in a sweeping sigh. So many land together that the tree looks and sounds alive.

'A starling tree,' Simon smiles.

'Yes, city birds with nowhere else to go.'

'There you see, I told you it would just be kids messing around.' He squeezes my hand.

I look around at the gang. In the twilight the boys are like the birds; roosting in the dark anonymity of the city, noisy and restless, jostling and wrestling together.

At that moment Spider sees us. As agile as a monkey, he jumps down from the statue and lands in our path. His cruelly short hair glints in the evening sunshine as if his head is coated with metal. He is wearing the current uniform for yobs, baggy black trousers and an enormous T-shirt that nearly reaches his knees. Despite his small stature his face is as taut and mean as a stray dog's. Something about him reminds me suddenly of the vixen in the garden. He has wildness and cruelty stamped all over him. I'd never realised before that Spider is not really domesticated.

Simon goes to walk around him. But Spider does this exaggerated sideways leap and once again is in front of us.

'It's the creep with the jeep.' Spider leers at Simon. 'Givvus your car keys and I'll move your motor to a safe place. You can't be too careful with them soft tops. Very easy to get into and nick. Gimme the keys and I'll take care of it for you. I'll do it as a special favour like, 'cos your slapper's bro's a friend o' mine.'

Simon looks so bemused I don't think he has fully understood Spider's broad accent and street jargon. But he knows trouble when it is parked right under his nose. His hand in mine is suddenly clammy, and I know he is afraid.

A wave of protectiveness towards Simon sweeps over me. I remember the cake and coffee set out on the kitchen table for me and the fortune he has just spent on a meal I have been unable to eat. He has done nothing to deserve this. And the one thing I can't stand is bullying.

Deliberately manoeuvring myself in front of Simon, I face Spider. He is about the same size as me so we are eyeball to eyeball. 'Eff off, Spider!' I say loudly. 'What are you going to do with car keys anyway? Pick your nose? You couldn't drive without a booster seat and a nappy.'

There is a ragged outbreak of mocking laughter from the assembled gang of boys. I can see that Spider is taken aback by their lack of support. And I guess that the group is torn in their loyalty between Spider and Ginna. Abusing Simon is one thing, but I am different. By virtue of being Ginna's sister I am nominally one of them.

'Leave it out,' Ginna calls in a lordly fashion, and Spider backs away from me.

'Come on,' I say to Simon, gripping his hand tightly and walking quickly across the square. I am shaking now but Simon is fine.

'I take it that lot of nasties were from your school,' he says.

'Yes,' I mutter. I am too ashamed to tell him that one of them is my brother.

'Well, they didn't cause us any problems,' he says with satisfaction.

But he didn't see the look in Spider's eyes as we walked away. And Spider wasn't looking at Simon – he was staring at me. There was something cruel and hard in his look, and some primitive instinct tells me I will not come out of this spat with him unscathed.

Boys like Spider don't let anyone, and especially not girls, make fools of them without swift retribution following. I am so scared for Ginna I want to scream and wail. I want to get hold of my brother and wrap him in my arms and keep him safe. Instead I have to sit in the cinema and watch some crummy film that is full of car chases and gun fights. I close my eyes at all the violent bits because the faces of the actors turn into Ginna and Spider and it makes me want to cry.

I'm so taken up with misery and worry that I hardly notice Simon squeezing my hand for all he is worth. He also keeps buying me popcorn and Coke, none of which I can touch.

It crosses my mind that Spider might have got the gang on his side and they will be waiting for us outside the cinema. But the square is empty apart from a couple of drunks lolling on benches and shouting at each other.

The birds have settled. They are safe for the night – the starling tree whispers with their presence. But at the edge of the concrete box one lost bird crouches, hunched and terrified. I pull away from Simon and pick it up. It has been injured, clipped by a car, or struck by a missile. 'Poor little thing,' I say, stroking its back. 'It's still breathing.'

'Give it here,' Simon says. He take the bird from me, and with one swift movement breaks its neck. Then he throws it into the rubbish bin and brushes his hands together as if anxious to be rid of any trace.

'Why did you do that?' I ask, anguished.

'Its back was broken. It was the kindest thing to do. Anyway it was only a starling...' He is astonished by my upset.

'How did you know how to kill it?'

We never kill anything at home, not even spiders or

earwigs. Pa says earwigs are the best of mothers. I wonder if that starling was a mother, a father or an offspring.

'I go shooting with my uncle. I promise you that bird didn't feel a thing,' he says boastfully. 'Honestly Fawn, it was kinder than just leaving it to suffer.'

'I was going to take it home. My brother's good with animals,' I mutter, trying not to cry.

'It was *only* a starling,' he says with disbelief.

We walk in silence. My hand in his is limp and chill. Seeing Simon kill the bird is like some kind of omen. I feel full of fear. I am so worried about Ginna I'm almost breathless with panic.

'You will come out with me tomorrow, won't you, Fawn? It's my last day before I am sent back to that prison of a school. Please?' Simon asks. His voice is light-hearted but there is a thread of seriousness in him too.

'Say you will, please?' he says again, as we edge through the dark city streets and on to the ring road. Before I can answer there is the blare of a horn and a small red car zooms in front of us, nearly clipping the wing of the jeep. Simon swerves and swears. Then he says: 'It's those crazy kids from the square. They want locking up.'

Instantly I am alert, gazing intently at the red car which is rocketing away from us. 'It can't be them,' I whisper hoarsely. All I can see are bobbing heads and the rear lights flashing. 'They're not old enough to drive.'

Simon shrugs. He doesn't care. But my heart is fluttering so much I feel dizzy. I want to ask him if he is sure, but my throat is so tight and dry I can't speak.

'Tomorrow then. Say two o'clock. I'll collect you. OK?' he asks insistently. I am too numb with worry to disagree. I don't care about anything but Ginna. I keep on praying that Simon has made a mistake.

Outside our house Simon cuts the engine. Then he reaches across and kisses me awkwardly at the corner of my mouth, his lips rather wet and sloppy. It reminds me of being licked by the dogs earlier in the day. He seems more nervous now than when we faced Spider earlier in the evening. And I wonder how many girls he has kissed before. I would guess not many.

'You really are the most remarkable girl, Fawn,' he whispers, his eyes brilliant black in the street lights as I move away. He doesn't try to kiss me again. I get the feeling he is a bit frightened of me.

'See you tomorrow,' I say wearily, as I jump down from the jeep.

Once inside the house I race up to Ginna's room. But the bed is unmade and empty. None of my prayers has been answered. He isn't home and he isn't safe. I don't know what to do. For a time I sit on the edge of his bed and cry. Then, cold and weary, I curl up in my own bed and force myself to stay awake. The night is full of sounds; the far-off city roars like some dangerous wild creature, and nearer at hand there are voices, cars and cats wailing. I wait longingly for the bang of the back door and Ginna's footsteps on the stairs, staring blindly into the darkness.

4

The last time I look at my clock it is midnight. Then, the next thing I know, it's morning and my bedside lamp is still on. Fear fills me up, sloshing around in my stomach, making me feel sick. Racing into Ginna's room I yank back the grey flannelette sheet. He burrows into the pillow like a creature disturbed during hibernation.

'Go way... leave me alone...' he mutters, pulling the sheet back and trying to move away from the light. Gazing down at his unwashed face and greasy tousled hair I'm awash with a mixture of relief and fury. He stinks of alcohol and fish and chips. The big question is where he got the money for these things when he hadn't been into work.

With a mutter of annoyance I get hold of his shoulder and shake him awake. He is still wearing the football shirt he was in last night and his jogging bottoms have been thrown on the floor.

'You filthy beast. You've slept in your clothes! You are going to have a bath and then talk to me! Ginna, this is important.'

'Bog off.' He shrugs my hand away. 'You sound like someone's mother.'

'Listen,' I hiss. 'Ma's got a bad ankle.'

'So? Not my fault. What do you want me to do about it?' he says, with a pathetic attempt at cockiness which reminds me of Spider.

'She's still got to work. She is out every day clearing up after rich people's brats. The last thing in the world she needs is to worry about you.' My memories of the Charles' home and how they treated me fuels my rage. 'You selfish little pig! Just because we live on a run-down council estate and go to a pit of a school doesn't mean we have to be delinquents.'

'Get lost...' Ginna opens one red-rimmed eye and sneers at me. 'I was just out having fun. Like you do with your posho boyfriend. What do you expect me to do? Stay around here all the time to keep you happy?'

'Have you been stealing cars with Spider?' I ask in a rush, because I'm afraid of the answer. 'Tell me the truth Ginna, have you?'

'Leave me alone. I'm tired,' he mutters. And he slumps back down, snuggling under the pillow. Either he is feigning slumber or is totally exhausted. Either way he is not listening. The floor is icy under my feet and I'm shivering.

Pulling back the curtains I find that summer has disappeared and, like my gloom-laden mood, the world outside is heavy and dark. Downstairs Pa is hunched over the gas fire and Ma is busy cooking. All the windows of the house are steamed up like it's winter.

'You're all dressed up. Are you going out?' Ma asks, looking rather anxiously at my best jeans and jumper. Chewing my lip I mumble something about a walk with Simon after lunch.

'It's not much of a day for walking,' Ma muses. And I stomp out and slam the kitchen door. I hump my school bag up to my room. Soon it will be time for exams and, up until now, I have wanted to do well. Now my enthusiasm seems all washed up, just like the solid sheets of rain bouncing off the tarmac road. If I go to the sixth-form college there will be no one else from Meadowlea. It had seemed like an adventure when Adam was going, but now it seems like a penance. My holiday job at the supermarket, where I have an identification number, a till and a voucher for the staff canteen, seems infinitely preferable to being at school.

Ginna doesn't get up for lunch. Ma carries his food up on a tray, as if he is ill. The three of us eat in silence. Two o'clock arrives but Simon doesn't. Ma smiles at me sympathetically and makes me a cup of cocoa as a consolation prize. I take it upstairs to my room, muttering about finishing homework. The reality is that my books are still in my bag.

Sitting down on my bed, sipping the cocoa, I try to work out how I feel about Simon not turning up. This is the first time I have ever been stood up and the sensation of rejection is surprising sharp, even though I don't particularly like Simon. I realise that what I was really looking forward to was going to Ilkley Moor and seeing the dogs again, and this disappointment has made me irritable and angry.

When I try to get into Ginna's room I find he has pulled the chest-of-drawers in front of the door and will not listen to my whispered entreaties. My head feels ready to explode with pent-up rage. The thought comes to me that I can go to Ilkley Moor by myself. I have the money Mrs Charles gave me and there will be a bus from the centre of town. I'm a free spirit – I don't have to wait around for Simon or Ginna. This idea is so alluring that I walk out of the house without saying goodbye to anyone, glad to be free from them all for a while.

It's great getting on the bus and just going somewhere different. When Ginna and I were little kids, Ma and Pa used to take us to Bridlington on the train, just for the day. That excited holiday feeling comes back to me as I slowly eat a bar of chocolate and watch the rain sliding down the bus windows. It is pouring so hard I can't see where we are going but I don't really mind that. The bus jolts and stops endlessly, rocking me to sleep like a drowsy baby in a pram.

Eventually the driver turns around and shouts to me: 'This is the end of the line. Do you want to get off here or are you going to pay me the return fare and go back to the Interchange?'

'Is this Ilkley?' I ask slowly, peering out at rain-washed grey buildings looming through a heavy mist.

'Of course it is. This isn't a bloody mystery tour. Move it, or I'll miss my break,' the driver snaps.

Turning up the collar of my coat I hunch my shoulders against the rain and wonder why everyone is allowed to be rude to the young, at the same time vowing that when I am grown up I won't do it.

To begin with I hang around the town centre, dodging into shop doorways to get out of the rain. Some of the shops are open and I go into a bookshop for a while. But the woman behind the counter keeps on giving me these long hard looks, as if she thinks I'm going to pinch something. Even when my back is turned to her, I can still feel her eyes following me.

After leaving the bookshop the rain slackens off to a light drizzle. I am sick of looking at things I can't afford to buy. So I stop an old man and ask where the moor is. He seems amused by my question but points me in the right direction. The route he has shown me on goes through the town, then up a very steep hill, and by the time I reach the top I'm sweating and breathless.

There are some really huge rocks standing like a natural castle on the brow of the hill. In the mist and drizzle they look sinister and spooky. It would be good fun if Ginna or Adam were here with me, but I feel a bit nervous about walking up over the moor by myself.

There's no one around and it seems weak-minded to turn tail and walk all the way back into the town, so I begin the long slow climb up towards the rocks. A couple of startled game birds rise up in front of me, flapping away with a strange cat-like cry. They make me jump like a nervous kitten and I am tempted again to turn back, but it's still early and I have nothing else I want to do. So I carry on, climbing right to the top.

It is while I am crossing a small stream, jumping from rock to rock, that I realise I am really enjoying myself. The hard walking has made me warm and now the rain has stopped my jeans have started to dry. Concentrating on walking takes up all my thoughts so my worries are forgotten.

Eventually I walk right around the big rocks and on to the top of the moor. It's brilliant! When the mist clears, a great panorama of hills and valleys is spread out before me. It feels like I am alone on top of the world.

Tiredness comes upon me suddenly. My legs begin to ache and then to shake and my throat is suddenly tight from thirst. The idea of drinking from one of the small springs which run down the hillside comes into my mind, but I think better of it. The realisation that I have to walk back across the moor and all the way down to the town hits me. Searching through my pockets I retrieve a greyish Polo mint and suck it to take the edge off my thirst.

Using the big rocks as a guide I turn and retrace my steps. Now the rain has stopped the larks have started to sing, and the moor is full of their trilling song and the rushing sound of water cascading in the streams.

Suddenly, underpinning the bird song and water noise, there is a different sound. It is faint but makes me stop and listen. It is a whimpering cry, like a small creature in distress. It stops suddenly, as if I have imagined it, but then starts again. I follow the sound for ages and end up walking around in circles. Sometimes the noise tails off and I think maybe I'm going crazy from lack of water like people on desert islands. It comes again and again, sometimes faintly, sometimes louder. It is a sad little cry that could only be ignored by someone with a heart of stone.

Eventually I realise that whatever is making the noise is hiding and doesn't want to be found. Crouching down and feeling a bit of a fool, I begin to call and talk to what ever it is. Eventually I give up because my legs are really stiff and aching now. A cup of tea and a hot bath seem like the most wonderful things in the world. With a shrug I set off down the hillside, but then I hear the noise really close by. Stepping off the path I search among the bilberry bushes until I locate the source of the whimpering.

I find myself looking down at a small dog. It is impossible to tell what colour it is because it is absolutely lathered in mud. It cringes away from my hand and begins to lick at one of its front paws – the pads are red raw as if it has been running on hot coals.

Moving slowly, my voice no more than a whisper, I scoop it up. 'You're only a baby! I wish Ginna was here because he would know what to do with you.' The puppy is limp in my hands, so cold I wonder if it is dying. Stifling a shudder I slip it inside my coat. It doesn't struggle but lies like a damp stone against my chest. 'Don't die on me. Ginna will love you. I'm going to take you home to my bro,' I whisper encouragingly.

In the car park the refreshment kiosk is open. Carefully counting out my money I buy a cup of tea in a polystyrene mug and a bar of chocolate, which I share with the pup. It licks every trace of chocolate from my fingers with a warm pink tongue and snuggles contentedly against me.

'What you got there, lass?' asks the woman in the kiosk, leaning over the counter and staring at me.

'A puppy. I found it under a bush. Someone must have abandoned it.'

'What a shame. Poor little thing. We get all sorts left up here. Had a litter of kittens left in a bin bag the other week. Wicked, isn't it? Tell you what, there's a lady in the town runs an animal shelter. She'll take it in. She finds good homes for them all. It's a bonny little thing, isn't it?'

The puppy is now warm and heavy in my arms. I have got used to the dampness and wet-dog smell of it, so I don't want to put it down or be parted from it.

'My brother loves dogs. I'm going to take it home. He'll be able to look after it. He's ace with animals.'

'That's nice.' She smiles encouragingly at me. 'Do you want a refill?' Before I can shake my head she adds kindly:

'Have it on the house.' She refills my cup with tea and hands me two KitKats. 'They're nearly out of date. You have one and give the other to the pup. Keep you both going for a bit. The poor little thing must be starving.'

Putting the pup down on the grass I break the biscuit into small pieces. Then the kiosk lady and I watch the pup eating like two fond surrogate mothers. Before I can thank her properly, lots of climbers arrive and start ordering hot dogs. Eventually I just wave goodbye to her, even though she isn't looking, and set off for the bus stop.

Even though I hide the dog inside my coat until I am sitting on the bus the beady-eyed bus driver spots it. When we stop at the traffic lights he calls out to me: 'Here, you at the back. It's half-fare for dogs.' The eyes of everyone on the bus swivel to where I am sitting.

'How come? It's not taking up any room,' I say sulkily. My fiver is seriously eroded and I will need to buy a collar and dog food for the puppy. I need to pay an extra half-fare like a hole in the head.

'Because, stupid, there's two of you. You and the dog. One ticket for you. One for the dog. Pay up or get off the bus.' This bus driver is even nastier than the earlier one. Being called stupid makes me feel really cross.

'But I've paid to go to the Interchange,' I argue. 'You can't make me get off now. It's a stupid rule anyway. Do you make pregnant women pay twice because there's two of them?'

One or two people on the bus laugh at this remark and an old man sitting in front of me says loudly: 'Bloody little

Hitler, get on with driving the bus and leave the kid alone. It's only a scrap of a dog.'

That remark really riles the bus driver. He pulls up at the next stop with a jerk. We all fly forward. Because I am holding the puppy I crack my shoulder against the seat in front. There are furious mutterings from several of the passengers. Some of them are grumbling about me, some about the driver, who is marching down the bus towards me. 'You kids are nothing but a bloody nuisance! Now pay for the dog or get off. And I want no more lip from you.'

Red-faced and embarrassed I count out the half-fare. Then the driver goes back to his seat and we set off. After that a stony silence descends upon the bus. Some people smile at me sympathetically but several give me hard stares. It is with great relief that I eventually get off and begin the long walk home. The puppy is now warm and dry, but getting restless.

Some instinct tells me I must hurry if I want to see Ginna, and despite my aching legs, I walk as quickly as I can, thankful that we live at the bottom of the hill. The afternoon is drawing to a close, and I know that Spider gathers his gang together in the early evening. They will have been stuck indoors all day because of the rain and will be desperate for some kind of activity. A few years ago they would have spilled out of doors and raced up to the rec to play football, but now they seek different pleasures.

I get to the top of our street just in time to see Ginna mooch across the road. His hands are in his pockets and his collar turned up – he is going out on the town. I am too late! In desperation I begin to shout his name and try to run. But the weight of the pup and my exhaustion make me hobble like an old woman. Hearing his name, he turns furtively, and when he sees me he breaks into a sprint and disappears. My steps falter and I blink back tears. Then, because I am so tired, I sit down on the kerb and lower my head down to the pup, sunk in a cloud of misery because my bro has run away from me. I think back to when we were little kids and were so close it seemed like we were one person split in two. We shared all our joys and sorrows and Ginna never knowingly hurt me. Now he's ripping me apart and he doesn't care. Tears run down my face and drip off the end of my nose and chin. I am too tired and despondent to search for my hanky so I rub my face on my sleeve.

My head jerks up like a puppet when I hear my name. Ginna is scowling down at me. 'What's the matter with you? What are you doing sitting down there?' he asks roughly. Swallowing my tears I open my coat. Nestling next to my filthy jumper is the puppy. I don't speak. I just watch as Ginna's brown eyes narrow and then widen, and his deep frown begins to lift. 'Where did you get it?' he asks.

'Found it. It's a stray. Been abandoned.'

'It looks as if it's been underground. Did someone try to bury it?' He sounds really angry now, but not with me; his anger is for whoever might have ill-treated the pup.

'No. I found it on the moor, maybe it's been down a rabbit hole. What shall I do with it?' I ask pathetically.

'Well, it needs a wash for a start.' He is stroking the puppy's head with one finger and a tiny seed of a smile has been planted at each corner of his mouth.

'Do you think Ma will let us keep it?' I ask anxiously.

'Dunno. Maybe if we offer to pay for its food. Do you want me to take it?' His hands are reaching for the puppy. I try not to grin too much but my heart is singing because he has said 'we'. Miraculously I've found something in the world which is more important to Ginna than being in Spider's gang. My eyes fill again as I watch Ginna place the pup inside his coat with all the tenderness of a midwife delivering a baby. Then we walk slowly home together.

There is no hot water at home, but I wash my face and hands and put on a clean jumper and some dry socks. Then I make a big pot of tea and a plate of toast. Ma is out. According to her note, Mrs Charles arrived after I left and asked her to work because they'd had unexpected visitors.

Minutes tick by and I keep expecting Ginna to hand the pup over to me, but he seems totally absorbed. He washes her and makes her a baby dinner of Weetabix and gravy. And while he is doing this he decides we should call her Solo, because she was found all alone.

'I'm a bit worried about her paws, they're very sore. I'll put some Vaseline on them, but I think she needs some antibiotic cream,' Ginna says.

'We could take her to the charity place in town. That's free,' I say. 'And we'll have to get her a collar and lead.'

'I'm skint,' Ginna says gloomily.

'I've got a bit in my post-office account, we'll use that.'

The kitchen door bangs and Ma comes in. She looks around at the mess in the kitchen: the dog-bath, the cardboard box in which Solo is sleeping and the table cluttered with our plates and mugs.

'For heaven's sake,' she cries. 'What on earth have you been doing? It was tidy in here when I left, now it looks as if a bomb has hit it.'

'We've found a puppy,' I say eagerly. 'Look, isn't she gorgeous?'

Ma sighs. 'You can't keep it. You better take it down to the police station or to the RSPCA.'

'Can we keep it if we promise to look after it?' I beg desperately.

'Oh, it's not that, it's the pigging money,' Ginna says, tight-lipped. 'Isn't it?' he asks, with a scowl in Ma's direction.

'Yes, as a matter of fact it is,' Ma says sadly. 'I hardly earn enough to feed and clothe us without a dog to look after. It's not just the food,' she says as I try to interrupt. 'It's the vet bills. And the mess in the house.'

My chin is trembling with trying not to cry as I begin to clear the table. Ginna looks down at Solo, curled up on his old jumper inside the box. 'I'm off out,' he says.

'Oh, Ginna!' I wail. 'Don't go out. What time will you be back?'

'Dunno,' he says, shrugging off my restraining hand. The door bangs shut.

I turn to Ma. 'There, see what you've done? You've spoilt it all!'

Ma ignores me and starts to tidy the kitchen. From the sitting room comes the sound of Pa's record player. He is singing along to a Bob Dylan song. I feel delirious with temper. I have to get out of the house. So I pull on my jacket and place Solo inside it. She is warm and soft and smells of shampoo and I am filled with love for her.

'Where are you going, Fawn?' There is anxiety in Ma's voice.

'I'm taking the puppy down to the animal charity shelter.' I don't add that I have every intention of bringing her home again.

'Well, that's all right,' Ma says. 'Will you get the bus?'

'Yes,' I mumble.

'There's some change in my purse, use that for the bus fare,' Ma says kindly.

As I take the money from Ma's purse I feel like the ultimate form of low life. But I am really tired and can't face walking into town. Confusion overwhelms me because I have always thought that love was a good emotion. It's been part of my upbringing to believe that. But the love and protectiveness I feel towards the pup is making me do bad things. I don't understand it and neither can I stop it.

The volunteer is just closing up the animal centre, but she smiles at me and unlocks the door. 'What have you got there? Isn't it gorgeous!' she says. I explain about finding Solo and how sore her paws are.

The woman gently examines Solo, gives her an antibiotic injection and hands me a tube of cream. 'Use that twice a day. It's important to keep her paws clean. Don't let her walk in the street, keep her on grass and away from other dogs until they've healed. You'll also have to trace her owner,' she adds.

I swallow what feels like a cannonball of spit from my mouth and croak: 'She's a stray, someone left her out to die...'

'Oh, I don't think so.' The woman looks down at Solo, who is standing on the table. 'I would imagine she's got a fantastic pedigree. She's a beautifully bred Border Terrier. I should imagine she's made her paws sore running around trying to find her owner. Terriers are very devoted as a rule.'

'She's a mongrel,' I say almost aggressively.

'She certainly is not,' the woman says, smiling. 'Now, dear, don't get too attached to her. There will be a worried owner out there looking for her. Take her down to the police station and give them all the details. If you want to look after her until she's traced I'm sure they'll let you care for her. You may find she's got an identichip, most breeders use them these days. A vet would be able to tell you.'

This woman looks like some harmless old granny with her grey hair and baggy cardigan – and she has been like an angel to Solo, who is looking up at her and wagging her tail – but I feel a surge of real hatred towards her. 'What's an identichip?' I mumble.

'A microchip under the skin. It can't be removed and it has an owner's details on it which can be read by a scanner.

Bring her back in two days' time, if you've still got her, and I'll check those paws and give her another jab.'

'Do I have to pay you for the cream?' I ask, scooping Solo up and putting her inside my coat.

'No,' the woman says kindly. 'But you do have to promise me to go down to the police station.' She waits for an answer. I stand, sullen and silent, until the silence in intolerable.

Then I mutter: 'I'll go, I promise.'

'There's a good girl,' the woman encourages me. And I turn away in case she sees the anger and despair in my eyes.

Exhaustion and bad temper make me walk very slowly to the police station. It takes me hours. With each step I grow more miserable and more child-like. So by the time I arrive at the cop shop I resemble a manic depressive six-year-old. I zip my coat up and tuck Solo out of sight. She is fast asleep, cuddled to my stomach like a baby marsupial to its mother.

There is this real old, grumpy sergeant at the desk, and when I stomp in and let the door slam he sighs and leans on the desk. 'And what can I do for you, then?' he asks curtly. I stare at him, unsmiling.

'Wanna report a lost dog.'

He reaches under the counter for a pad and sighs again. I bet he is wishing he'd worked a bit harder and made it into the CID. 'And where did you lose this dog, exactly?'

'Didn't lose it. Found it.'

Another sigh. 'Right, so you've found a dog. Have you brought it with you?'

'Nope.' I stare at the counter.

'Why not?'

'It's only young and it pees all the time. I thought it would pee on your floor.' I shift my gaze from the counter to the floor.

'How very thoughtful,' he murmurs with heavy irony. 'Right. So where is this lost dog?'

'At home. Wanna keep it there.'

'Where exactly did you find it?'

'Kind of near the Harrogate Road...' I mumble. For some reason I do not want to tell this fat policeman that I found Solo on Ilkley Moor. I suspect he will ask why I had gone there. The truth seems to stick in my throat like a piece of accidentally swallowed chewing gum.

'Where exactly on the Harrogate Road?'

I backtrack and begin to describe various roads. He stabs a fat finger on the map of the area on the wall behind him. 'The Otley Road, near there, I think,' I say with relief.

He scribbles busily. 'Now describe the dog.'

'Small, scruffy, black.'

'Breed?'

'Dunno.'

'Probably a Heinz 57,' he says knowledgeably. 'Male or female?'

I say female, but by this time my voice is so low he mishears me. I watch him write MALE on the form and my heart is hammering in my chest. 'I dunno, really,' I add lamely.

'You're a bright 'un, aren't you?' he says irritably. 'Don't they teach you kids anything in school these days?' He looks down at my name and address. 'Which school do you go to?'

'Meadowlea,' I say sulkily. He doesn't reply but makes a 'humph' noise in his throat which speaks volumes.

Relief makes me clumsy and I nearly fall out of the door of the police station. My conscience is throbbing and pricking and my face burns from all the lies and half-truths I have told. And I have to keep thinking about Solo, and Ginna's face when he first saw her, to blot out the knowledge that I haven't told the truth to the policeman. 'Wasn't my fault he was deaf,' I mutter to myself. 'Silly old git.' And at least I can tell the old woman at the animal centre I have reported finding Solo. Over and over I repeat to myself: she didn't have a collar, she's a stray. It is like a mantra and it makes me feel a bit better. By the time I reach our road I have nearly made myself believe it.

5

Monday morning isn't like a normal day in our house. Ma has relented, just like we hoped she would, and allowed us to keep the puppy. So the first thing which happens is that Solo wakes us very early by barking when the milkman arrives. Ginna gets up immediately and takes her up to the woods, which is utterly amazing because normally he needs a wet flannel around his ears to move him from the bed.

The next surprise is that a package arrives for me. The postman shoves it through the letter box and it rests on the worn rag-mat by the front door like an unexploded bomb.

We never get any post – apart from bills in brown envelopes which Ma hastily pushes behind the clock on the mantelpiece. On our birthday Ginna and I get a birthday card each with a bank note inside, from our Granny and Gramps in Ireland, Ma's parents. Pa's parents stopped speaking to him when he dropped out of the orchestra and they never send us anything – not even a Christmas card. So the arrival of this parcel is a mega event in our house.

Ginna picks it up. 'Parcel for Miss Fawn McKenzie marked personal and private! Must be from Posho.'

Snatching it away I snap: 'He's called Simon,' and disappear into my room. Simon must have gone to the sorting office to have got this delivered so quickly. It has got all kinds of stickers on it and *Priority Posting* in red letters.

Inside is a wad of paper all covered with wonderful italic writing and a book of love poems. The book has Simon's name in the front and is fairly well-worn. Dropping it on to the faded counterpane on my bed I skim the letter. Firstly he apologises for not turning up and begs me to forgive him. His mother took away his car keys and refused to let him out because his godmother had called unexpectedly. I don't know anyone else who even has a godmother so it sounds plausible to me. Then he tells me how he feels about me, and it's pretty passionate stuff considering we have only met twice and been out together once.

Although I can't help but feel flattered that he thinks I am special and tells me so at such length, there is also a nip of sadness tweaking at my heart. If I am honest, I don't really like Simon very much and I certainly don't feel like writing a lot of sloppy romantic stuff back to him. He also wants a photograph of me and has Sellotaped three pound coins to the bottom of the letter and asked me to go to the photo booth at the station. I sigh, wishing the letter had made me feel happy instead of manipulated and guilty. Then I quickly shove the letter, book and money under my mattress and pray that Ginna never finds them.

For a while the package takes my mind off going back to Meadowlea without Adam. I wonder how he is feeling about going to his new school this morning. For a few moments I am angry because he has escaped and I haven't. But it's hard to think badly of Adam – so I concentrate on the good times and how we survived Meadowlea together, and try to wish him well in my heart.

School is very different. For a start Ginna comes with me, instead of diving off with Spider and going into town. Also, the school has changed – the graffiti has been washed off the walls and the playground has been tidied up. There are even new litter bins and tubs of flowers! I wonder how long the little pansies will last and how many days it will take for the bins, and the tubs, to be brimming with fag-ends and crisp packets.

Once inside the school, we find that the big clean-up has extended everywhere. The floors are gleaming and the whole place smells of paint and polish. There are teachers I have never seen before who marshal us into the school hall. They aren't unfriendly, just very brisk and efficient. The hall is laid out with chairs and we are all made to sit down. There is a new raised dais at one end, like a stage, and a big burly, red-faced man sweeps on to it and introduces himself as our new Head. He gives us a pep talk about how the school is going to run from now on, about uniform and behaving properly.

The new Head is nearing the end of his speech. We have all started to fidget in our seats, when I suddenly get this nasty feeling creeping up my neck – just like when you are watching a horror film on the telly and you get really scared. Turning around I find Spider sitting behind me and staring at the back of my head so hard his eyes are glazed with concentration. It is unbelievable that he is finally in school. The authorities must have been on to his parents. A shudder runs through me. It would have been a better start for Meadowlea, and for me, if he was nicking off.

The new head – Mr Backhouse – comes into our first lesson and gives us another pep talk about being the GCSE group and the flagship of the school. He tells us the eyes of the world will be on our results and that we must work hard. There is an unnatural silence from Spider and the rest who would normally play up, but then Mr Backhouse has a tough face and very big beefy hands.

Our next lesson is music. We trail across the playground to the music annex expecting to be told to do some private study or reading. But the music rooms have been transformed. The walls are covered with posters – stuff about bands and orchestra. There are also musical instruments in there – drums and keyboards, as well as a big tape-recorder and CD player on the desk. I hope the teacher will remember to keep the annex locked because Spider will be working out how much all this stuff is worth. There is a second-hand shop in town which will take anything.

The teacher is waiting in the main music room. He is asking the kids their names and telling them to sit down in the chairs which have been set out ready in a semi-circle at the front. Because I am trailing at the back of the group, I hear his voice before I see him. And I respond like Solo does to the sound of Ginna and me. There is something in the quiet authority, the pitch and tone, which makes me feel good. I find myself relaxing slightly. This guy sounds like he is in charge. I still have terrible memories of the humiliation of the last music teacher. Watching Spider baiting teachers can be pretty horrible – like watching an animal being hunted and then hurt. Today I feel sad enough without Adam. I don't want anything else to make me feel down.

The new music teacher stands before me. His voice makes him sound like a very powerful person, but he looks very ordinary: light brown hair, blue eyes, a taut intelligent face. He is not very tall and rather skinny and is dressed in casual trousers and a checked open-necked shirt, the kind cowboys wear.

'Hi,' he says to me. I am the last one in. He takes a quick look at the clipboard in his hand where he has a list of all our names. 'You must be Fawn McKenzie. Come on in and sit down, Fawn.'

His smile transforms his face. It takes away the slight tension in his eyes and the rather moody set of his mouth. It is a smile which not only reaches his eyes and makes them crinkle, but spreads out, like the rays of the sun, and envelops me in a feeling of warmth and well-being. It is as if I am moving in slow-motion as I walk across the room in front of him. It is the strangest, newest, most mind-blowing experience. I've never felt like this before or been struck by this overwhelming desire to get to know someone. Suddenly I want him always to smile at me, just like that, so welcoming and kind.

'Come and sit down, Fawn,' he says again, and he moves across and kind of shepherds me into the last seat. I sit in a daze staring at him, studying him intently. He is not the most good-looking guy I have ever seen – Adam is taller and more handsome – even Simon is more striking. But he just seems completely right to me. Everything about him is perfect and knowing this makes a lump come into my throat.

He introduces himself: his name is Ben Thompson, which is a very plain kind of name. And I wonder why the sound of it seems to burn itself into my mind. He is giving out pieces of paper. We have to write down what kind of music we like – groups, bands, anything. He also wants to know if we play any instruments or are interested in learning. When he gives me my bit of paper I see that my hand is shaking. A strange fear fills me because I have been so scornful of Simon and his sudden passion for me, all the time thinking how silly it is – not believing it is possible to see someone for a few moments and know for certain that you are in love with them. Now I know the truth. Love can hit you like a runaway ten-ton truck and there is nothing you can do to avoid it.

Staring dumbly down at the paper I remember a Shakespeare play we read in English, where a magic potion is used which makes you fall in love with the next person you see. I wonder if Simon and I both got stardust sprinkled in our eyes. Finally, just before the forms are collected in, I scribble something down.

The gang is starting to play up. Grinning and leering at each other, and led by Spider, they start singing a rugby song. 'Thought it was music, sir. Thought we was meant to sing,' Spider says with a knowing wink. Ben Thompson just turns and looks straight at him and then he addresses the whole group as if Spider has not spoken.

'Right, you lot, shut it will you? We've got something else to do,' he says. His voice is not raised but there is a note of firmness in it which indicates he is not going to be pushed around. In the moment of silence, before they can begin singing another song, Ben presses the button and a blast of music erupts from his tape machine.

The class explodes with laughter. Ben switches it off. 'Recognise it?' They all shout out the product which the music helps to advertise and some of them sing the chorus. 'Right, now try this one.'

He keeps up the pressure. It is like a quiz game. The other kids don't realise they are studying music. They think it's just a time filler. Gradually he slows down the pace. He starts to ask questions. 'Why do you think they chose that piece of music? What does it make you think of when you hear it?'

The class is rowdy but fun. Two people don't join in. One is Spider. He is sitting slumped in his chair, his chin touching his chest, pretending to be asleep. His gang is ignoring him and he doesn't like it. And the other person is me. I just sit and watch Ben, too taken up with my rollercoasting emotions to think about telly adverts.

'Now this is a difficult one. Don't shout. Just listen.' Unbelievably, the class is quiet. The music rolls out. Ben turns to me. 'Any ideas, Fawn?' I jump as if startled.

'I don't know,' I say, playing for time. Part of me wants to get the answer right, but part of me wants to hold on to this moment, when Ben Thompson is looking straight at me and waiting for me to speak.

Just at that moment Spider plays the oldest trick in the book. He throws a handful of biros and pencils down on the floor. The gang is immediately on hands and knees, shouting out as if they are little kids: 'Spider's dropped his pencil case, sir. He's lost his pen.' The girls start shrieking 'cos they know what happens when Spider's gang is crawling around on the floor.

Spider is on the floor next to me. 'No point asking Fawn McKenzie anything. She's one sandwich short of a picnic, just like her old man.' His face is twisted with some awful mixture of mirth and dislike as he lunges under my chair. I feel his hand, hot and sweaty, pinching the soft skin at the back of my knee. It's incredibly painful and shocking in its suddenness and something inside my head snaps – like an elastic band stretched too tight and then let go.

'You little shit!' I scream. 'Don't you dare touch me with your filthy paws, you animal!' Suddenly I am out of control with rage and pain and, without even realising what I am doing, I pluck him out from under my chair and smack his face with the full force of my body. He keels over but is instantly back on his knees and grabbing me, his fingers kneading into my flesh. Again I scream, and for a moment we are rolling on the floor like a pair of wild creatures. I am sobbing with a mixture of fear and anger as I grapple with him.

Suddenly, he is lifted off me. Ben Thompson and Ginna have got hold of Spider's arms and Spider is screaming with pain. The air is filthy with Ginna's snarls and swearing. But it is nothing compared to the rage on Ben Thompson's face which burns like white fire. When he speaks his voice is no more than a whisper, but pent-up emotion vibrates through the air. 'Don't you dare treat a girl like that in front of me,' he breathes. He jerks his face away from Spider, I see that he is almost overwhelmed by his feelings. 'Class dismissed. Get out, all of you! River, look after your sister. I'll be back in a minute.' Then he sweeps Spider out of the room as if he is a piece of trash that needs to be got rid of quickly. I drag myself into a chair and cover my face with my hands. Ginna puts his arm around me, tries to say something, then moves away to the window, as if unable to cope with my misery.

'I can't get her to stop crying,' he says, when Ben comes back into the room.

'It's all right, River. She probably needs to cry.' Ben crouches down in front of me and I feel his hands on mine; they are soft and warm and very gentle. He is trying to put a big clean cotton handkerchief into my hands. But I can't look at him or get my fingers to work. 'Come on, Fawn,' he says gently, and he mops my face and pushes my hair out of my eyes as if I'm a little kid.

'River, Mrs Jessop is making Fawn a cup of tea. You can have one too if you like. Would you please just pop across to the office and collect the tray?'

'Yeah,' Ginna says, scooting out the door as if glad to get away from my awful outpouring of grief. I am crying for more than a physical skirmish with Spider and the end of my clean record card at Meadowlea. I am crying because I have fallen in love, and lost any chance of ever making that person love me, all in the space of an hour. If you could die at will I would just expire there and then. There seems nothing in the world worth living for.

'Fawn, Fawn. Please stop crying. Would you rather talk to Mrs Jessop than to me?'

'No!' I say, shaking my head violently. 'I don't want to see anyone else. Please don't make me.'

'All right, just take some deep breaths and try to stop crying. Please, for me...' he begs. I risk a little look at him. He is still crouched in front of me, his hands hovering, as if he would like to hug me but doesn't dare.

Pressing his hanky over my face I force myself to stop sobbing. The hanky smells so fresh and clean; I concentrate on that and the comfort of Ben's nearness.

'Good girl.' I can hear the relief in his voice. 'Did he touch you very badly, Fawn? Do you know what I mean? I need to know because, if he did, I will have to take this further and call in the police.'

'No, it wasn't that, so much – not that I like having Spider's grubby hands anywhere on me. I just wasn't expecting to be hurt for no reason.'

'I can understand that,' Ben says quietly.

'It was such a shock. He's never tried to bully me before. Ginna, River, is in his gang... I wish he wasn't,' I add forlornly.

'Poor Fawn.' His voice is so kind that my tears spill again. He pats my shoulder and then sits on the seat next to me. 'Here's Ginna with the tea. Good lad. Look, he's even got some biscuits out of Mrs Jessop. He must have plenty of charm.' He takes hold of my hand and places a cup and saucer in it. 'Come on now, Fawn. Drink this,' he says firmly. 'I can promise you things are going to improve around here. You won't have to put up with this again. Not in my lessons or anyone else's. I give you my word.'

I risk a glance at him. He is drinking his tea and watching me. I look away quickly. 'I've never been in trouble before,' I say, my chin wobbling dangerously.

'I know you haven't.' He pats my shoulder again. 'Cheer up, there's a good girl. I know it wasn't your fault.' He turns away and starts asking Ginna what music he likes. I drink the tea and listen to his voice, which is very soothing. Ginna tells Ben he plays the guitar a bit. Ben goes into the store cupboard and finds him an instrument to try. And then suddenly, to my astonishment, Ginna starts telling him all about Pa playing firstly in an orchestra and then in a band.

'You're good on that guitar. Maybe we could get a group going. I notice that Richard Ekheart plays the drums,' Ben says, and he sounds really excited. Not like a teacher at all.

'Yeah, and Fawn sings. She's got a great voice,' Ginna says, swept away by Ben's obvious enthusiasm.

'I haven't...' I croak.

Ben turns and grins at me. 'Tell the truth,' he says, just as if we are a couple of kids talking.

'Well, I sing a little bit...' I admit.

'Tomorrow, lunchtime. Meet me in the hall – both of you? Please?'

'Yeah,' Ginna is striking chords on the guitar. 'Nothing else to do. I'll come along.'

Staring at Ben, my eyes feel raw with crying, and now I want to start all over again. I know that now he has said 'please' to me and looked into my eyes I cannot say no. He has me in thrall. I wonder if he has any idea of the power he has over me. Minutes before I wanted to die, and now I can't wait for tomorrow lunchtime.

'Would you like to go home?' Ben asks sympathetically. 'You and Ginna can cut class. I'll make it OK with the office.'

Ginna and I look at each other. Outside the sun is shining. 'We've got a new puppy,' I say slowly. I know we are both thinking of taking Solo up to the woods, maybe taking a sandwich and spending the whole day there.

'Well, you get off and have fun with your dog. And just remember, Fawn. Tomorrow is a new day.' He smiles into my eyes and surprisingly I find myself smiling back.

'Hey, Ginna,' Ben says, as we are gathering up our bags. 'Have you got a guitar to practise with?'

Ginna's face colours. 'No,' he says slowly. 'Pa doesn't play any more.' He doesn't say that Pa sold all his equipment to buy stuff to smoke.

'I can lend you that one. Keep it safe, OK? And bring it in tomorrow. I'm always here early so you can leave it here during lessons.' He goes back to the store cupboard and gets a guitar case for Ginna. 'See you tomorrow, Fawn,' he adds and I can only nod, my heart is too full to speak.

'He's great, isn't he?' Ginna says, as we make our way down the hill. 'Hey, Fawn. What songs do you want to sing?'

Shaking my head I say quietly: 'I don't know.' But in my heart I know I will sing songs of love and longing. Sad songs about unrequited love. Songs about kids who have no hope in life but their own mad dreams... I may even write a song of my own because there is a melancholy melody going through my mind and when I think of Ben all kinds of words start to swirl around in my head. I begin to hum the melody and Ginna joins in.

'Cool song, Fawn,' he says. 'Just right for a funeral.' And I thump him with my school bag and keep on singing.

The next morning another letter arrives from Simon. There's about six pages of it. Most of it is love poetry which I cannot read without crying. I think how simple life would be if we were all in love with the right people. There is Simon vowing that he can't live without me, and I am feeling that too, but not about him. I expect Ben Thompson is madly in love with some snobby girl, who in turn is in love with some other guy. Though I find this hard to credit, I kind of hope it is true, because the idea of him having a fully-requited love affair with some girl shoots arrows of pure jealousy into my heart.

At school we are all marshalled into another assembly. Mr Backhouse is in full throttle and bellowing at us about manners and behaviour. There is no sign of Spider. Everyone is staring at me. I wonder if Spider's gang will pay me back but they are all looking a bit green and sickly and I get the feeling that Mr Backhouse has dealt with them. None of them will look me in the eye.

As we are leaving the hall Ginna says to me: 'He won't be coming back. He was on his last chance. I reckon he's gone to one of them units.' I don't know what to say. Sorry doesn't seem appropriate.

It doesn't seem possible that Ginna will come to the rehearsal with me and I am too scared to contemplate going on my own. Despairingly I watch the gang congregating around him, like he is heir apparent and about to be crowned King now Spider is dethroned. They're treating him like a hero. So why should he turn his back on them and spend a lunch break with his sister and Richard Ekheart?

Richard Ekheart, Ekky as he is known, is not the kind of kid you want to hang around with. To survive at Meadowlea you either have to be in with the roughs and make your mark, or you have to be invisible. Ekky is one of the invisible ones. He is a big strong lad, with pale blue eyes and thick corn-coloured hair, but I don't think I have ever heard him speak more than two words together. He's perfected the art of being moving wallpaper and kept out of trouble.

To my delight Ginna seeks him out at the end of morning school. 'Coming to the rehearsal, Ekky?' he asks. At first Ekky's face is totally blank as if Ginna has not spoken. 'Me and Fawn are going,' Ginna adds, and suddenly Ekky's face breaks into this big grin. It is definitely the first time I've seen him smile. He doesn't reply but follows us, like a lumbering blond bear, down to the main hall.

Ben Thompson is waiting for us: he has set up electric guitars, the drum kit and a microphone for me. It is like suddenly being a pop star, and my stomach tightens with tension and pleasure. He doesn't hassle me about singing. They do some messing around, Ginna on guitar and Ben on keyboards. Ekky is surprisingly good on drums. He goes into a kind of trance when he plays. You have to jump up and down to make him stop. I sit and watch them. Finally,

I get a bit edgy. They are all enjoying themselves and I think maybe Ben has forgotten about me.

Then he turns and smiles at me and any irritation or anxiety just melts away. 'Come on Fawn...' he encourages. 'Tell us what you want to sing.'

'Do the reggae you like,' suggests Ginna, and we arrange the key it's in, who is playing what and work out all the words. At first my voice wobbles all over the place. But then, to my amazement, Ben begins to sing harmony with me; and I am so thrilled to hear our voices blending together and soaring out across the hall that I lose myself completely in the song.

'You've got a great voice,' Ben says, with a big grin at the end of the number.

'Sing that song we tried out yesterday, sis,' Ginna says. 'She makes up great songs,' he adds proudly.

'Shut it, Ginna,' I say, my face growing hot. It's one thing singing a song you've written to your twin, quite another to sing it to the guy who was your inspiration.

'I'll hear it when you're ready to sing it to me, Fawn,' Ben says, and I duck away so he can't see my eyes.

Rehearsing during lunch breaks and after school becomes my addiction. Ben makes it such fun that Ginna, Ekky and I are all completely hooked after day one. Other people get drawn in by the insistent thump of the music which echoes around the entire school like Morse code. Other kids start to drift in, mostly in twos, like animals coming in to the ark. Ben doesn't hassle them. We are not used to relaxed teachers at Meadowlea and it takes a bit of getting used to. He says they can do what they want, watch or join in. The only rule is that there is no messing around or distracting the band. Most of the kids don't play any instruments but Ben finds them easy things to play or encourages them to sing. It's wonderful to watch him drawing people out and making them feel confident.

Finally, after about two weeks, I sing my song for him. I choose a day when it is just the four of us in the hall, but even so it is totally terrifying to sing a tune and words I have written myself. I cannot look at Ben as I sing about having a heart that is breaking into a million pieces. It would be awful if he should see the truth in my eyes.

When I finally dare to shoot a glance at him, I see that he has a little frown on his face. 'That is a very sad song, Fawn,' he says slowly. 'A real tear-jerker. It really suits your voice.'

'I write happy songs too,' I say quickly, because I want to see him smile at me. And then I sing this song Ginna and I wrote together about Solo, which is a really cool. I have another song which I have written that I have to keep secret. It is about Ginna and how happy I am he has stopped hanging around with Spider. It has a verse about Solo, and another about making music together. Ginna would kill me if he heard it because it's so sentimental and kind of religious. But it's also true – Solo and music have turned out to be his salvation.

It's then that Ben makes his earth-shattering announcement. 'I think we're nearly ready to plan our first gig. How about one evening here in the hall?'

'What, sing for people?' I gasp.

Ben laughs, 'Why not, Fawn? You've all got lots of talent. Why shouldn't people want to hear you? Especially singing original material.'

'I'm not singing *Heartbreak* for anyone else,' I protest.

'Fawn, creative people write in order to show it to other people. You may think now that you write these songs for yourself. But one day you'll realise you do it to share. But when we are rehearsing, if you feel you don't want to sing your own material that's fine. We'll just do some reggae and pop. Songs you all like.' He looks at me and smiles, and I realise that, if he wants me to sing my song, I will, because I would do anything in the world for him.

'Any chance of a weekend rehearsal?' he asks. 'I don't think the caretaker will let us in here. But my parents have a barn we could use. I could pick you all up Sunday lunchtime here at school?'

We all nod and agree a time. And I have to keep telling myself not to smile so much because I'm afraid of looking ridiculously happy. It seems unbelievable that I am going to see Ben's home and spend nearly a whole day with him. I have to pinch myself to make sure I am not dreaming.

'Oh, bring your dog with you, if you like. There are lots of dogs at home for her to play with,' Ben says when we are leaving.

When we get home I write to Simon and tell him about the rehearsal. He has taken to writing to me every day which is a major embarrassment at home. I have to ambush the postman and try to get the letters before anyone else sees them, but I can't always manage it and then Ginna gives me hell. And all these letters put a great strain on me because I feel I have to write back. Obviously I can't reply with all that romantic stuff he sends to me so I have taken to sending him a kind of diary.

So he knows all about school and Ben, whom I always call Mr Thompson. Sometimes I feel like a spy from an old film working behind the Iron Curtain and sending out misinformation to cover my tracks. Because you would think that the Mr Thompson I write about is at least forty and wears a tweed jacket. But I can't very well tell Simon my true feelings – that I am madly and hopelessly in love with my teacher and not with him. And I can't face writing about anything else. Whereas writing about Ben, the things he's said and what we have done in rehearsals, is wonderful.

So I quickly scribble an account of my day, which opens with *Hi Simon*, and ends with *See ya soon, luv Fawn*, and dash to the post box to catch the last collection. Not very lovey-dovey but Simon doesn't complain. He keeps sending me books of first-class stamps and begging for more.

The post box is next to the phone box where I tried to ring Adam. I stop for a moment and think about him and how uncomplicated life was when we were together. I seem to have lived a hundred years since the beginning of term. My life has turned upside down but I have never been so happy. That's what love does for you.

6

Ben comes to our house when we don't arrive for the rehearsal. I suppose the school must have a record of our address, or maybe Ekky knows where our house is, though I don't know how or why he should.

The police car outside doesn't deter Ben. He comes straight up to the front door and rings the bell. I know it is him – from the front-room window I can see his car piled high with the drum kit and instruments. Ekky is sitting in the back, looking straight ahead, as if he is on a different planet to the rest of us.

Reluctantly I make my way to the front door. The thought of facing Ben makes me shiver deep inside with dread. I am all cried out and my eyes are dry and sore from all the tears I have shed. I open the door, not wide, just a crack.

'Fawn, can I come in?' he asks.

'I suppose so.'

He slips in through the door and closes it firmly behind him. He can hear the voices in the kitchen so he sidesteps me into the front room. 'What's going on? Can I help?'

Hanging my head, I am unable to look at him. 'It's the puppy I found. I thought she was a stray but the owner reported her as stolen. The owner is here now with the police.'

'Oh Fawn! I'm sorry. How...?'

I know what he is going to ask. 'The woman at the animal shelter who gave us some medicine put her on a lost and found register. She's very valuable.'

The voice in the kitchen becomes more raised. 'Is that the owner?' Ben asks. I nod. 'Do you want me to stay here?' he asks. I nod again. 'Give me a shout if you think I can do anything to help,' he adds.

In the kitchen, Mrs Blenkinsop, the owner, is still standing in the middle of the room shouting her head off. She is quite young and pretty, but her face is screwed up into a frown of annoyance and her voice seems to be getting louder by the minute.

'This wretched girl has caused me weeks of worry and expense. My husband and I have scoured the countryside looking for Sophie. We have covered every inch, every inch, I tell you, of Ilkley Moor.'

'Yes, so you've told us, several times,' says the young WPC, who has come along with Mrs Blenkinsop. She is trying very hard to hold on to control of the situation, but no one can get a word in edgeways.

'It's Mr Thompson, our music teacher from school. We're late for rehearsals,' I say loudly.

'That's a shame, isn't it?' Mrs Blenkinsop says rudely. She turns to the WPC. 'Well, what are you going to do about all this? Are you going to charge her with something? Or will it just be a warning? I tell you frankly, I want something done! It's cost me money; not just the time and effort, but in petrol too.'

Pa has been standing behind Ginna. No one has taken much notice of him. Everyone has been too busy staring at me. I am the sixteen-year-old who is too dumb to know a boy dog from a girl dog. The girl who is too ignorant to know a pedigree dog from a stray. The nuisance who kidnapped Mrs Blenkinsop's prize puppy and whisked her away from Ilkley Moor while Mrs Blenkinsop was shouting and whistling and searching. But now Pa steps forward. He is quivering a bit, but his eyes are very focused and searingly blue.

'Just a moment, madam. I would like to say a word. I have stood here and listened to you calling my daughter a thief and a liar. We have heard your version of events but can we please, in the interest of justice and fairness, hear another viewpoint?'

I hang my head. It is unbearable to see him, his trembling fingers knotting in his beard, trying to justify my completely idiotic behaviour.

'We *have* asked Fawn,' the WPC says, looking at the clock rather deliberately, as if we've already taken up too much of her valuable time. 'And she doesn't seem to remember very much.' She doesn't add that I have stood like a sulky child and answered in monosyllabic whispers.

Pa turns on her furiously. 'And why should she remember? What significance did any of it have for her? None at all. She was out for the day. She was busy enjoying herself. I tell you, Mrs Blenkinsop, I am proud of my daughter. When she found a dog that was muddy, frightened and lost, she didn't turn her back or pass by on the other side of the road. No, she was a Good Samaritan. She stopped and took care of the animal. Fawn has been raised to treat all God's creatures with respect and kindness. But as for her not being sure where, or even when, she found the dog, this shouldn't be held against her. The important fact is, she did find the dog. Solo was lost and Fawn brought her home, washed her, fed her and cared for her. And Fawn reported finding the animal to the police station. If the officer didn't get the pertinent facts down correctly then he is at fault. He is the professional adult.'

'The desk sergeant can sometimes be very brusque and it's easy to make mistakes when you're busy,' the WPC adds quickly, before Mrs Blenkinsop can speak.

'Quite so,' Pa says. 'Fawn was sure the dog was a stray, so maybe getting the facts right didn't seem very important to her.'

'Humph,' Mrs Blenkinsop says, scowling at me.

Pa looks at her, long and hard. I have never seen him like this. He is so assertive and confident and the words just spill from his mouth as if he is a lawyer or something.

'And now to the assertion you keep making that the dog was definitely found on Ilkley Moor. Have you, as a dog breeder, never come across the situation where an animal, if severely frightened, will set off at a run and keep moving in a straight line? This is a well documented fact of animal behaviour. And before you accuse my daughter of lying, you would do well to remember that. Solo could have been found anywhere. I suggest you should be prosecuted for allowing a young dog, without a collar, to be running on the road, which could have caused an accident. You should be very grateful that someone as responsible as Fawn came along and rescued the dog.'

'Sophie wasn't on the bloody road!' Mrs Blenkinsop shouts at him. 'I've told you – she went down a rabbit hole on the top of Ilkley Moor. It's miles away from any road!'

'And presumably Solo came out of that rabbit hole, but you didn't see her, did you?' Pa says, his words coming out like a rapier thrust. 'You didn't find her, so how do you know where she came out or where she was found?'

'That's quite true,' the WPC says quickly. 'And obviously Fawn has looked after the little dog very well, you can't deny that, Mrs Blenkinsop. I think maybe it would be best if you thanked her for that and we left.'

'Thank her?' Mrs Blenkinsop yells. 'I'll do no such thing.'

Pa looks at her as if she is something bad in a dustbin. 'You talk about your expenses. What about the food and collar that Fawn has bought for the dog?'

'I don't want any money for looking after her,' I say quickly. 'I love her.'

There is a sudden silence in the room. Everyone is looking at me. 'I wanted to believe she was a stray because I loved her from the moment I saw her. She was so cold and small. I put her inside my coat and she was just like a baby.'

Sitting down at the table I hold my hands out to Ginna. He takes them and I see his mouth moving. 'Please just go,' I whisper. I can see that at any moment Ginna is going to cry and I can't bear for it to happen in front of the young bored WPC and hateful Mrs Blenkinsop.

Ginna looks up. His face is all screwed up and his voice is a croak. 'If we pay you for her, would you let her stay with us... Please?' he adds.

'Certainly not,' Mrs Blenkinsop says. 'This isn't a fit home for a dog.' Ginna puts his face in his hands. Mrs Blenkinsop turns to the WPC. 'I expect you could find all kinds of things if you had a good look round here,' she adds nastily, eyeing Pa with disdain.

'Look, I came here to find a lost dog. I haven't got a search warrant. And, as your dog has been perfectly well looked after, I suggest we leave.' The WPC's face is all pink and cross. She obviously resents being told how to do her job by Mrs Blenkinsop.

Mrs Blenkinsop goes 'Humph,' and marches across to Solo, who has been sitting curled on Ginna's lap. She pulls the puppy to the floor. Ginna doesn't move. Solo whines and pulls away from Mrs Blenkinsop; she obviously wants to go back to Ginna. Mrs Blenkinsop's face is like a thundercloud as she clips on a puppy harness and lead and snaps: 'Walk, Sophie.' Solo won't walk and Mrs Blenkinsop picks her up. 'Lost all your manners,' she says huffily.

'She doesn't want to go,' I say.

'Nonsense,' Mrs Blenkinsop says, and stalks from the room. The last sight I have of Solo is her little black and ginger face peeking around Mrs Blenkinsop's arm. Solo looks puzzled and rather frightened. She will be so lonely tonight because she has got used to sleeping with Ginna, curled up on his chest so she can hear his heart beat.

The silence in the kitchen is heavy and sad. I am very sorry to have lost Solo, but now fear has started to filter into my pain. The fear that now Solo has gone, there will be nothing to keep Ginna at home and he will go back to Spider's gang. I go over and touch his shoulder. 'Mr Thompson's here. We're meant to be going to his house to rehearse.'

'OK,' Ginna whispers.

When I go into the front room Ben is standing looking out of the window. He turns quickly and says angrily: 'She yanked that puppy down the path. It obviously didn't want to go. Why didn't she just leave it here with you?'

I shrug. 'We're ready to go, sorry to have kept you waiting. Thanks for coming down here.'

'That's OK.' He moves across and looks down into my face. 'I'm very sorry about your dog.'

'Yeah. Well, I'm all right. But Ginna...' Words fail me. What can I say to describe Ginna's pain?

'Come on, then. Let's get going. He'll need something to take his mind off it,' Ben says. We go into the kitchen. Pa shakes Ben's hand.

'You've got two very talented children,' Ben tells him, and Pa smiles with pleasure. I wish I could tell him how proud I was of him for the way he stood up to Mrs Blenkinsop.

'Are you OK to rehearse?' Ben asks Ginna.

'Yeah...' Ginna says. He goes across to the sink and fills a mug with cold water and downs it. Then he splashes his face and rubs it dry with the tea-towel. Now it doesn't matter that his eyes are red.

Ekky doesn't ask why the police were at our house and Ben talks about music as we drive out of the town. When we get past the suburbs and the big supermarkets, out to where there are fields and trees, Ginna seems to wake up. 'Where are we going?' he asks.

'My parents' farm just outside of Kierley.'

'What kind of farm?' Ginna asks.

'A bit of everything, mainly dairy and sheep. But Mum keeps hens, ducks and geese and she breeds Border Collies.'

'Oh,' Ginna says. Then he adds: 'Solo was a Border Terrier but we didn't know.'

It's awful the way he's talking about her in the past tense – as if she's dead. But I suppose she is for him now.

'She looked a lovely little dog,' Ben says. His voice is gentle.

'Yeah, she was,' Ginna replies gratefully. And I realise that he wants to talk about Solo, whereas I just want to blank the affair out of my mind. I suppose it's because I feel that the whole sorry mess is my fault.

The farm intrigues me because it is Ben's home. It is a long low stone building with narrow windows. Outside is pretty scruffy, with piles of wood and old bits of machinery. This cheers me up. I'm glad it's not absolutely immaculate like Simon's house. As soon as you get out of the car you can smell the animals.

Ginna takes a deep breath and smiles. 'Will we have time to see the cows?' he asks tentatively.

'Yes, if you want to. Come on in. Mum said she'd have some lunch ready for us.'

Ben's mother is like something out of a storybook. She has grey hair swept up in a bun, twinkly grey eyes and a soft downy unmade-up face. She is wearing a summer dress and a big pinafore which is streaked with flour.

'I was just getting worried. Come in, how nice to meet you all,' she says, as if we are welcome visitors and not just a load of scruffy kids who have come to rehearse in the barn. She fusses around us, shows us where the cloakroom is so we can wash our hands, and then sits us down at the big kitchen table and fills us with food. There's egg and bacon pie, salad, bread, cheese and two different kinds of cake. Everything is home-made and Ginna and Ekky eat an embarrassing amount between them. I try to kick Ginna under the table and give him a meaningful look as he reaches for a third piece of cake.

Mrs Thompson laughs and says: 'It's grand to have lads to feed again.' And she tells me about Ben's two older brothers and elder sister. I get the feeling she misses having kids around the place. I can't imagine why Ben is so thin when there is all this food at home.

A tall man, who looks like Ben, pops his head around the door. 'Still at lunch?'

'They were late arriving, dear,' Mrs Thompson says.

'Well, I need a bucket of hot water and a towel. I'm having trouble with that cow. Calf's got its legs all tangled up.'

'Is it being born?' Ginna asks through a mouthful of cake. My foot connects with his leg and my look says: 'Don't speak with your mouth full.'

'Well, it will be if I can get it straightened out.'

'Can I come and see? Please?' Ginna asks.

'You'll not have to get in the way or make any noise,' Mr Thompson says a bit brusquely, and Ginna's face darkens.

'Oh, he'll be a help. He can hold the towel for you. I'll find you some wellies. Come on, Ginger,' Mrs Thompson says soothingly.

Mr Thompson's head reappears around the side of the door. 'Ginger, what sort of name is that?'

'It's 'cos of me hair,' Ginna mutters.

'Well it's not ginger, it's red,' Mr Thompson says with a grin. 'Come on Red. I'm concentrating on the cow so if you faint you're on your own. Get a move on.'

Ben and Ekky go out to the barn to set up the equipment and leave me with Mrs Thompson. 'It's a lovely house,' I say, looking around. The kitchen has a big Rayburn cooker with a box of wood next to it. There are two old armchairs on either side of the range and a small television on the Welsh dresser. It's easy to imagine Mr and Mrs Thompson sitting in here in the evening.

'Would you like to look around?' Mrs Thompson asks kindly. 'I love looking around other people's homes,' she adds with a grin. And I can see where Ben gets his wonderful smile from. He looks like his dad but he smiles like his mum.

'Oh, yes please,' I say, wondering if she would be so friendly if she knew the reason I am fascinated by the house is because it is Ben's home and if you are in love with someone you want to know everything about them.

Ben's mum takes me into the sitting room, which is very tidy with a piano in the corner and old-fashioned embroidered mats on all the tables. 'We don't use this room much now all the children have flown the nest. We make an effort and light the fire on a Sunday. But during the week we live in the kitchen. Of course when they were all at home I used to keep it warm so they could do their homework in here.'

She leads me into the dining room, which is rather dark and full of bookcases. 'We only use this room at Christmas time. It's a bit of a waste really, isn't it?'

Immediately I am riveted by the pictures arranged along the length of the sideboard. There are some of the whole family – it is easy to tell Ben because he is the youngest. But I also pick him out from among the single photographs. 'That's Ben, isn't it?' I ask, reaching out my hand but not quite touching the silver frame.

'Yes, looking clean and tidy for once. He was a terror. Always in trouble and always dirty. Not that you'd know it now.' Mrs Thompson laughs and reaches into the sideboard drawer and pulls out some baby photographs. 'Here he is at a year, and again at five. His first school photograph.' I lean over her arm and drink in the sight of the young Ben.

'Wasn't he beautiful? He looks like an angel,' I breathe. 'When did his hair turn brown? He was so fair then.'

'Oh, when he was about seven. I think he did it by wishing so hard. He thought having blond curls was very sissy.' She looks at me and smiles sympathetically.

'Do you think you can make things happen by wishing very hard?' I ask, watching sadly as she puts the photos back in the drawer.

'Yes, I think sometimes you can, if you want it badly enough. Look, I've got lots of copies of the baby photo, the photographer gave me a whole sheet. Would you like one?' She scrabbles around in the bottom of the drawer and finds the photographs. 'They're all slightly different,' she adds.

'He looks lovely in all of them,' I whisper, my heart so full of gratitude I can hardly speak. She cuts the corner photograph off the sheet and hands it to me. It has a slight dent in one corner, but for me it is the most precious thing in the world. 'I won't tell him, or show it to anyone,' I say, conscious suddenly of my face growing hot. 'I hope if I ever have a baby he looks just like this,' I add, slipping the photograph into the pocket of my jeans.

'That's a lovely thing to say, Fawn.'

As we leave the room I manage to stammer out, 'Thank you very much, for the photo, Mrs Thompson.'

'That's all right, dear. It was the sort of thing I liked to have when I was your age,' she adds kindly. And I wonder, with a little lurch of despair, if she has sussed out how I feel about Ben. I am terrified that it might be obvious to the world, although I have been very careful to hardly look at him since we've been here.

Ben is waiting for me in the kitchen. He smiles and says: 'We're all set up and ready to go. We're playing at the end-of--term disco at school, Mum.'

'That's lovely dear, I might come out and have a listen later on.'

Ginna bursts into the barn when we are warming up. 'I cleaned the calf. I got the gunk out of its mouth and nose and it started breathing,' he announces. I haven't seen this expression on his face for years. He looks all lit up like he did when he was six and we got Merlin from the RSPCA.

Ekky pulls a face but Ben smiles and says: 'Well done! Are you going to join us?'

'Yes, I will,' Ginna looks a bit shamefaced. 'But I did tell your Dad I'd help him with the milking, if you said I could. He says his lad hasn't turned up. I've never done milking before.' Ginna looks down at the borrowed wellies and tries to hide the delight on his face. 'Is that OK?'

'Yes, sure. We'll do your pieces now and then Fawn and I can work on our songs. We could do with a long session on vocals,' Ben says with easy good humour.

Mr Thompson puts his head around the barn door about an hour later. We have just finished. As soon as he sees Ben's dad, Ginna is pulling off his guitar as if he can't get away fast enough.

'We'll break for a drink, shall we?' Ben asks Ekky and me. I watch Mr Thompson and Ginna stomping across the yard in their wellies. They are deep in conversation and Ginna looks totally at home.

'He's not really a city kid at all, is he?' Ben asks softly, and I know we are thinking the same thoughts.

We sit outside to have our tea. Ekky walks around the garden looking at the flowers. Ben and I sit on a bench together. I feel as if the photograph is burning a hole in my pocket and I have to keep my hand over the place to make sure it's still there and hasn't slipped out.

'You and Ginna know a phenomenal amount about music,' Ben says. 'I am amazed by the songs you know. It's really good, Fawn.'

'Yeah. Well. Pa plays music all the time. Other kids learnt nursery rhymes. Ginna and me learnt the words to Van Morrison songs.'

'Have you thought about taking a GCSE and then maybe studying music at college? You play guitar and piano, don't you?'

'Well, I've never had any proper lessons. I play by ear.'

'Have you thought about what you want to do, when you leave Meadowlea? Term will be over in a few weeks. Once you've taken your exams you don't have to be in school at all. I'll suppose I'll have to try to put a new school group together. But you'll be a hard act to follow.'

He smiles at me, as if I should be flattered or pleased by his words. But I stare at him with horror. It is terrible to have it spelled out to me that soon I won't see him any more. There will be no more rehearsals, no more time together when I can watch his mouth and wait for his smile. I suppose in the back of my mind I had thought that the group would carry on, that we would all still be together. Now I know the truth.

I stare down at the grass sulkily, ignoring my mug of tea and hot scone. 'I was going to try for the sixth-form college but I don't want to go now. I think I'll get a job...'

'You could take Music GCSE and A level at evening class,' he says. 'I'll get the prospectus for you, if you like?'

'Yeah, I'll think about it,' I say miserably.

'Your dad will be knocked out when he hears you singing, Fawn. He'll be so proud of you,' Ben adds. 'Sometimes in rehearsal you move me to tears. You are very talented. Singing from the heart is something you can't learn. It's a gift.'

My eyes fill. I am still trying to reconcile myself to the idea that in a few weeks I will never see him again. 'Pa won't come to the disco,' I mutter.

'Well, that's OK. Maybe he would like to come to a rehearsal when we get to the polishing stage. It would be really helpful to have a professional to crit us.'

'He won't come to anything. There's a problem about him going out. He's ill.'

I glance at Ben. He is frowning and his eyes are stormy: grey-blue like the sea during a gale. He runs his hand through his hair as if he is distracted. 'I'm sorry, Fawn. I didn't know.'

'How could you know?' I say coolly. My heart is breaking and, with sudden unexpected cruelty, I want him to be hurting too.

'Teachers should know these things...'

'Should they? Why? What you gotta know for?' My voice is harsh, like the cry of a starling. And I sit hunched and terrified, a fledgling that has fallen from the safety of the tree.

'We need to know these things,' Ben says quietly, 'so we can handle problems with pupils. So we don't say the wrong thing.'

I can't bear to be reminded that he is my teacher and for him I am a job of work. That he can go back to school, read my school record, mug up on my family and know the rights and wrongs of my school life.

'He's got agra-something. It's no big deal,' I snap.

'Agoraphobia,' Ben says quietly. 'What happened, Fawn?'

'He got sick and stopped work, but he still went out. He used to go to the allotment. But the kids on the estate used to run behind him and call out, 'Old Peace and Love', and it really got to him. He started going less and less. Now he never leaves the house.'

'That must be very difficult for all of you,' Ben says gently. 'Does he have any treatment for it? Do you have a social worker or anyone to help?'

A little explosion of fear and anger erupts in my heart. I can just see a social worker snooping around our house, finding all kinds of illegal substances and calling in the police. Next thing you know, Ginna and me will be in care and Pa will be in jail.

'Look, we don't need a bloody social worker!' I whisper. 'We don't need anything. And I haven't told you all this so you can go into school and write it down on my record card. Or get the authorities breathing down our necks. I told you as a friend...' I stop, and suddenly I know that if I don't lose my temper I will begin to cry. 'You're just like all the others, aren't you? You're just a creepy do-gooder. I wish you'd never come to our school. I wish I'd never joined your lousy band. It would have been better if you'd just left us alone!'

Jerking away from his restraining hand I storm away to the bottom of the garden, past where the vegetables grow and down to the orchard. And when I look back, Ben has taken my untouched tea and scone and gone inside. I feel sick with temper and grief. Leaning against an apple tree that clings to the boundary wall, I close my eyes and feel hot tears pricking under my lids. Everything I said was true. I am hurting so much now that I wish I had never seen him. My life stretches ahead of me like a long weary road because I can't imagine living with any degree of happiness without him.

7

It is terrible to feel angry with everyone, even Ginna and Ben, the two people I love most in the world. Illogically I am angry with Ma and Pa too, so there is no one left. I suppose I have to face the fact that I am angry with the world, its creations and most of all with myself.

As we are getting into Ben's car to leave, Mrs Thompson comes out to say goodbye and asks cheerfully: 'Will we be seeing you all next weekend for another rehearsal? I do hope so.'

All I can manage is a wan smile. Ben's face is closed and moody and Ekky looks – well, like he usually does, as if the conversation is way over his head and not about him at all. It is Ginna who says with a smile, 'Oh yes, you'll be seeing me. Mr Thompson says I can come on Saturday and help with the sheep.'

'Don't you have a Saturday job?' Mrs Thompson asks

kindly, and I find myself scowling at Ginna as he shakes his head sadly. 'I'm sure he'll find you plenty to do,' she adds.

When Ginna gets into the car we find he smells absolutely disgusting. Even with the windows open the stink of silage and cows makes me want to puke. All he can talk about is the milking parlour and calves and what he will be doing the following weekend. It disguises the fact that Ben and I are not speaking – to each other, or anyone else.

'How are you going to get up there by five-thirty in the morning to start milking?' I ask eventually. It is a good seven miles from our estate to the farm. And it's the kind of place where there is only one bus a week. There is a long pause. Ginna looks crestfallen and I should feel sorry for him but I don't. I am just angry at him for being like me and having foolish dreams.

'I'll cycle,' he says.

'It's a fair old way – lots of hills,' Ben says glumly.

'I don't mind!' Ginna snaps.

I want to get hold of Ginna and shake some sense into him, but I manage to contain myself until we get out of the car. I mumble a thank you to Ben, without looking at him. But as Ginna and I walk up the pathway to the front door, I spit out:

'Which bicycle are you thinking of riding to Kierley? Your racing bike or your mountain bike?'

'I'll borrow Ma's bike,' Ginna says sullenly.

'You can't ride all the way to Kierley on Ma's bike! You'll never make it.'

117

'Wanna bet?' Ginna says with a shrug. 'Anyway, Mr Thompson's offered me a Saturday job and he's going to pay me by the hour. And more than stingy old Thomas ever did. I'll soon be able to afford a new bike.'

'If you don't spend it all on cider...' I snap.

There is a pall of gloom lying over the house as we walk in. Ma is at the sink, scrubbing her hands. This is her day off but she has spent it at the allotment, planting vegetables. I am not even sure if she likes gardening. But now Pa doesn't go down there someone has to do it. Ma's hair is falling over her face and I notice with shock that there are silver strands amongst the ginger. She isn't thirty-five yet – she is too young to be going grey.

Ma manages a weak smile. 'Pa told me about the puppy. I'm very sorry. She was such a dear little thing.' There is a long pause and then Ma tries to change the subject. 'Did you have a nice time? How was the rehearsal?'

We stand sulky and silent – both waiting for the other to speak. 'Oh, like that was it?' Ma says. 'Sit down, then. Tea won't be long.'

'Ma, can I borrow your bike next Saturday? It's really important,' Ginna says. There is the start of a whine in his voice as if he knows getting his own way will be uphill work.

'No! Of course you can't. You know I need it to get to work,' Ma says, rather irritably.

'Won't old Mrs Thing come and pick you up? You shouldn't be cycling anyway with that bad ankle,' Ginna says. He is too het up to be tactful. It all comes out like a complaint.

'There are lots of things I shouldn't be doing with this ankle. But I'm doing them anyway,' Ma says sadly.

'This is really important, Ma. I've got a job at Kierley and I need to get there early in the morning,' Ginna says desperately.

'Oh, don't be such an idiot,' I snap. 'Ma's got a job too.'

At that moment Pa appears in the doorway. From the front room comes the sound of Indian music and the sweet smell of incense. Pa's hair is ruffled as if he has just got out of bed. His face is pale and gaunt and his shoulders are stooped as if he is old. His eyes are not focused and I know, just by looking at him, that he is stoned. I can't bear him when he is like this. And all my good feelings about his bravery in defending me against Mrs Blenkinsop evaporate like mist in sunlight.

'River, Fawn, why are you shouting at your mother?' he says, holding his hands out to us. 'I have told you before that we must have harmony in this house.'

'River says he needs a bike,' Ma says with a sigh.

'Both these children live too much on the material plane,' Pa replies, shrugging his shoulders.

'Oh stuff it!' Ginna shouts angrily. 'I need a bike. It's important to me.'

'Well, you could walk if it's that important to you...' Pa says gently.

Ginna face twists with fury and, without another word, he turns and slams out of the back door.

'He'd be walking most of the night to get there at five-thirty!' I screech angrily, because now, suddenly and illogically, I am on Ginna's side against my parents.

'When I lived in Bristol I walked to the Glastonbury Festival one year,' Pa says dreamily. 'It was a real trip walking at night – no cars and no angry farmers. I followed the stars and went straight across country. It was wonderful.'

Ma carries on washing the vegetables, her shoulders hunched and miserable. I know it is best to ignore Pa when he is like this, but my irritation gets the better of me and I retort: 'He's got to work when he gets there. He'll be exhausted.' Recalling the expression on Ginna's face after he'd helped deliver the calf makes me want to scream at Pa. With an effort, through gritted teeth, I manage to grind out: 'Get real, Pa. You don't understand anything, do you? This is really important to him. He needs a bike.'

'Don't speak to your Pa in that rude tone, please Fawn,' Ma says automatically as she fills the kettle. And I realise that they are like radio receivers which are not tuned into my wave length. I am making sounds but they are just hearing emptiness.

'You two are utterly useless! You should never have been parents! You're too pathetic to live!' I scream at them. As I leave the house the last image I see is their shocked faces. Both of them looking at me with their mouths open.

I have to sprint to catch up with Ginna. He is making for the main road, walking quickly with his head down. 'Ginna, wait. Where are you going?' There is no Solo to keep him at home now or any chance of him starting the job at the farm. I have some idea of how desperate he must be feeling. It is terrible to really want something and know you can't have it.

'Leave me alone, Fawn. I'm going out with Spider. He's picked up loads of contacts at his new place. He's been begging me to go out with him. I can earn enough for a down-payment on a bike in one evening and then I won't have to do it ever again.'

'Don't be stupid! No one will sell you anything on the never-never. You have to have a job and a bank account. And Ma won't sign anything. You know what they are like about credit. If you go tonight you'll be in forever. And what happens if you get caught? There'll be no job on the farm then.'

Ginna doesn't even look at me as he says dismissively: 'Get lost, Fawn. Spider's got it all worked out. There's this window cleaner who sells the names and addresses of people who are on holiday. All we need is a motor. Spider's dead good at getting in and out of places.'

'Ginna! That's housebreaking. You could go to prison for years if you're caught. Please... listen to me. I'll find a way to get you a bike. But don't do this.'

We have reached the bus stop. I take hold of his arm, but he shakes me off.

'Look, all I want is a pigging bike so I can go to work. I don't want anything more. But I want that job and nothing is going to stop me. Not even you, Fawn. So just go home and stop making a fuss.'

Like a malevolent genie, a green bus appears. Ginna pushes me away, ignoring my tears and whispered entreaties. Everyone on the bus is staring at me; I am sobbing like a five-year-old. Ginna's face is blank as he hops aboard. The last I see of him is his copper-coloured head ducking down behind the seat to avoid my eyes.

I turn and begin to run. Not in the direction of home. There is no help to be had there. Now, driven by desperation, I am like a those city starlings circling and seeking a safe refuge.

It is difficult running uphill. I have to keep stopping and leaning over because I have a stitch. When I am about halfway to school I begin to cry, but crying takes up energy and makes it difficult to keep a good pace going. By an effort of will-power I stop and concentrate on running.

The gate at the back of the school is unlocked and I can see Ben's car parked by the door of the music annex. Relief makes me feel quite light-headed. I don't know what I would have done if I had missed him. I bang on the door and yell his name, and I see his puzzled face as he comes towards me. As he opens the door I fall into his arms.

'Hey, hang on, Fawn. What on earth is the matter?' He stands me on my feet and moves back slightly from me. My hands are reaching out for him, grabbing at his arm.

'Please, come and help me, Ben. Ginna has gone off with Spider to steal a car and go house-breaking. I know something awful is going to happen. Please come with me. I've got to stop them.'

'Do you know for sure where they've gone? Have they done this before?'

'Yes, yes. Come quickly.' I am pulling at his sleeve with impatient fingers. I am shaking so much I can hardly stand. Ben collects his car keys and locks the door of the music annex. He holds my arm as we walk across the playground as if I am an invalid or someone very old. The tears have started to fall silently down my face.

'Where are they?' he asks, as he starts the engine.

'Ginna got the bus into town to meet Spider. I think they'll go to the city centre car park. That's where I saw them before,' I say, through chattering teeth.

He doesn't speak, his face tense with concentration as he drives through the deserted city streets. But when we pull up into the car park we see that it is nearly empty – and there is no sign of Ginna, Spider or any of the gang.

Ben parks, then reaches into the back of the car and pulls out his fleece jacket and wraps it around my shoulders. 'Fawn, they're not here.' His voice is very controlled but his eyes are worried. 'They could be anywhere, couldn't they?'

'I don't know...' My frenzy has subsided. I am frozen with fear now, as if my heart has been turned into a block of ice and is slowly changing my blood to frost. I am as hard and cold as a glacier. 'I don't know...'

'Where did you see them last time?'

'Here early on and then in a car on the ring road.'

'Do you think they were going to some particular place or were they just riding around?' Ben's voice is quiet but intense.

'I don't know,' I repeat lamely.

'Fawn, I know you don't want to hear this.' His hand covers mine for a moment of comfort. 'The best thing would be to go to the police—'

'No!' I am rigid with terror. 'We can't do that, Ben. We just can't.'

'We'll try the ring road,' he says anxiously. 'We'll look for ten minutes and then it's the police. I'm sorry, Fawn.' I look at the determined set of his mouth and don't try to argue. At least I've got ten minutes to try to find Ginna.

The ring road is empty – it is a sultry summer's evening and the world is at rest. There are a few Sunday motorists driving real slow. And us, with the speedometer touching seventy miles an hour, acting like we are competing in a Grand Prix. Ben gets halfway around the ring road in ten minutes. There is no sign of Spider or Ginna. He starts to speak and I know he is going to say it's the police now, when we hear the distant waa-waa of an emergency ambulance and the blare of a fire-engine siren.

Ahead of us on the brow of the hill is a narrow line of smoke. 'Oh, Jesus Christ, please no...' Ben whispers, and it isn't swearing, it's a prayer. I sit as if turned to stone as Ben drives slowly towards the noise.

He slows down, and glances at me. Most of the drivers are turning off on to the slip road because it's obvious there is trouble on the road ahead. 'Fawn. Let me take you home and then I promise I'll come straight back and find out...' Ben begs.

'No!' I shout. 'I can't go home without Ginna!' And Ben flinches as if I have hit him.

A policeman stops us before we reach the accident. I can see the car. A big red Volvo estate mangled into the central reservation. Ben gets out of the car and speaks to the policeman. I can't hear what they are saying and I don't care. I have turned my back on Ginna once too often. This time I have to be with him. I wait until the policeman and Ben are deep in conversation and then I jump out of the car and sprint up the road to the accident. I don't get far before they spot me and I can hear them running behind me. 'Keep her away,' the policeman is shouting breathlessly, but I am demented with fear and they can't catch me.

I get to the ambulance and then I feel Ben's arms around me. 'Please Fawn, come away,' he is begging. I can hear the tears in his voice. I don't take any notice of him.

I look at the medic who is kneeling on the ground. 'I want my brother,' I say loudly. 'Where's my brother?' I look down at the stretcher. Spider is there, lying very still. He looks very young, like a little kid, and the dirt and blood on his face show up very clearly because he is so pale. They have a clear mask over his face so I know he is still alive. 'Spider...' I beg, and if Ben wasn't holding me I would bend down and shake him into consciousness. 'Spider! Speak to me. Where's Ginna?'

'He can't hear you, Fawn,' Ben says. I stop struggling with him and he takes hold of me and wraps his arms right around me so I can't see anything but his shirt.

'There was only one casualty,' the policeman is saying. 'There was only this lad in the car. He nearly crashed into an elderly couple on the Broadley roundabout just before he ended up here, and they have confirmed that he was alone in the car.'

Ben lifts my face with his fingers. 'Ginna isn't here, Fawn. He wasn't in the crash.'

'Where is he then?' I ask, broken.

'I don't know, but I promise we'll find him,' Ben says gently, as if I am a child who needs to be comforted.

The policeman wants to know who Spider is and where he lives. Ben says he can get all the information from school. We get back into the car and Ben says: 'If he was on the Broadley roundabout he had only just come on to the ring road. Let's try there first.'

Broadley is a suburb place with a row of a shops, a park and very little else. We ride along the main road very slowly. And then I see Ginna – he is sitting on the steps of the war memorial eating chips out of paper. I can't speak but I make some kind of inarticulate noise and then Ben sees him too.

We park in front of the stone cross and Ginna doesn't even notice us. I jump out of the car and race up to him. I grab the chips from him and throw them down on the ground and then I hug him until I can't breathe.

It is after this that my tears come like a torrent, so that I can't speak or even stand. Ben tells Ginna about Spider and they lift me into the car. After that everything is a blur. Next thing I know I am at home and Ma is helping me get into bed. I feel as if my mind and body are made from cotton wool. The only thing which is clear is the noise that comes through the thin partition which separates our bedrooms – it is the sound of Ginna crying. It seems to go on all night.

Ben comes to our house early in the morning. Ma has already gone to work and Pa is still in bed. Poor Ginna is finally asleep, his face buried in his pillow as if to blot out the horrors of the world, so I am alone in the kitchen. Ben looks awful. His face is unshaven and there are dark marks like bruises under his eyes.

'Could you make me some coffee, please Fawn? Strong and black,' he asks. He sits down at the table and stares into space. 'I've stayed with him all night, but there's no change.'

'Is it very serious?' I ask, biting my lip to stop the tears which are brimming in my eyes.

'He's on a life support machine. They are fairly hopeful he will pull through, though in what kind of state they can't say.' Ben shakes his head and his voice is suddenly angry. 'I don't know why they bloody well call it 'joy riding'. He's broken his body and head into a hundred pieces. They showed me the X-rays and it made me feel sick.' He puts his head down on his arms, hiding his face from me.

Taking hold of one of his hands I gently wrap it around a mug of coffee and then begin to make toast. 'I'll make you some breakfast. You should have something to eat,' I say uncertainly.

Ben raises his head and looks at me, his eyes dark as the night ocean. 'His house key was around his neck and they asked me to go to his home with a policewoman. They gave us a list of things they wanted: pyjamas, toothbrush, that sort of thing... Hospital policy, even if you've go no teeth or arms.

'And of course the police wanted to tell his parents about the accident. But there was no one there, Fawn. A neighbour says his Dad left about a year ago and hasn't been seen since and his mother had gone to Blackpool for the weekend. She goes there most weekends by all accounts.

'So we let ourselves into the flat. And Fawn, I doubt if Dean has ever had a pair of pyjamas or a toothbrush in his life. And, if by some miracle he did have, they certainly wouldn't be clean. The place was indescribable. There was nothing there – no food, no books, no comfort. Just a TV and lots of empty bottles. His mother's room was full of makeup and spilt nail varnish – her clothes were all over the floor. She lives there with him. But it isn't a home. It was just a place where people hang out. It...' Words fail him and he covers his face with his hands. 'I'm sorry. I shouldn't have come here and told you all this,' he says brokenly.

'I don't mind, you looked after me. I want...' I can't tell him all the things I want, so I move behind him and slip my hands over his shoulders. My touch is tentative as I lean my head over his until I feel his hair tickle my cheek. I want so much to comfort him. I want to wrap him in my arms and love and kiss all the pain away. But all I do is say in a calm voice, 'It's OK, Ben. You can tell me anything.'

'It just seems such a waste of time going into school and teaching music. Music – for God's sake! – when there are kids like Dean who don't have the basic essentials of life. What does music mean to him when he doesn't have a decent meal from one year to the next and lives like an animal in a cage? But I tell you what is worse than that! The fact that he has no one to care about him. There was no one there – not even last night when they thought he might die. Only me, a stranger.'

'No one ever said that life was fair,' I say softly, as I reluctantly let go of him and carry on making the toast. 'Some kids have a rotten life, but not learning music at school only makes it worse. At least you were there for him. You didn't say: "Oh I'm tired" or "It's not my problem". Some people wouldn't cross the road to help a kid like Spider, but you stayed with him. You can't blame yourself because the world is so awful. Pa says everyone should do any little good they can as they journey along life's highway. You do that in plenty.' I push the plate of buttered toast and a jar of peanut butter across the table to him.

'Have something to eat and I'll make you some more coffee,' I say in a fussy, motherly way to hide my feelings.

He looks up at me and smiles, a small tentative tremor of a smile, but a smile nevertheless. 'Thanks for the toast, Fawn. Now I smell it I realise I'm really hungry.' He reaches out and touches my hand. 'And thanks for the wise words.'

The smell of the toast brings Ginna down. He looks awful too, his eyes are really red and puffy. Ben is great with him because he talks him through what happened. About the argument he had with Spider and how he jumped out of the car at the traffic lights and went to the chip shop. It is obvious that Ginna needs to talk, but I can't bear to hear any of it. So I go up to the bathroom, wash in ice-cold water and sing hymns until they have finished.

Then we go to school and begin our revision and, at lunchtime, we have a rehearsal. Sometimes I see a sweat break out on Ginna's face and I know he is thinking about it all. And sometimes I find that the page I am reading suddenly turns into Spider's face: an eerily white, broken, little boy's face lying against the harsh grey of a hospital blanket. Then I have to shut my eyes quickly and drive it out of my mind. But Pa always says that life goes on like a river. And so I just go with the current and find that he is right.

8

Ginna and Ben visit Spider every night. I only go once. I am ashamed of myself because I am such a coward. But the hospital makes me feel really ill. I don't know how people work there. And I know I could never, ever be a nurse. Just the smell of the place makes me want to throw up.

Spider is in a small side room on his own, which I guess means he is still really ill. When we arrive his mother is there, sitting by the bed, leafing through a magazine. She wears lots of make-up and fake gold jewellery. It's hard to believe that Spider belongs to her; she's young enough to be his sister.

The room has lots of posters on the walls and a bright cotton cover on the bed with pictures of footballers on it. I guess that this is all stuff which Ben has brought in to brighten up the place because I can't imagine Spider's mother bothering.

When we walk in, she looks down at her long silver nails and says quickly: 'Oh well, if you're here for a bit, I'll get away now.' And she scoots off without even looking at Spider. It's obvious she can't wait to get out of the place. Not that I blame her entirely. I would run away too, if I could.

Ginna and Ben go up to the bed and take hold of Spider's hands. They start talking to him, taking it in turns to tell him what is happening in the world – stuff he would like, all about football and TV. The words just spill out, and I can tell they do this lots because they know all the things to say. I just stand and stare. It's so obvious to me that Spider, with his broken head, can't feel their touch or hear their voices but they do it all the same. Just in case.

I take a step nearer, knowing I should say 'Hello Spider' or something, but I can't speak or even look at his face. So instead I look at his hand, which is lying in Ben's palm. It is so white it looks green and all the veins are clear blue lines. Abruptly I take two steps back and feel a shiver begin inside me. I can't bear to touch him. And I can only marvel at Ginna, who is rubbing Spider's hand rhythmically, as if he is stroking a cat, as he gabs on about who is top of the league.

Very slowly, taking tiny steps, I back out of the room. Ben and Ginna don't even notice I've gone, they're concentrating so hard on Spider. If life is a river then I am on one side and Ginna and Ben are far away on some distant bank and I will never be able to cross this divide and get to them. I walk out of that hospital feeling lost and hopeless. When I get home I spend a long time looking at the baby photo of Ben and reading the book which Simon sent me. I need to lose myself in fantasy for a while. Reality is too hard.

When Ginna is not at the hospital he is at the Thompsons' farm. Ma relents and lets him have her bike. Ginna brings home green overalls that stink and wellington boots which have to be kept out in the shed because Ma says they are a health hazard. He also brings home magazines about farming and reads them – which is amazing, because, to my certain knowledge, he hasn't read anything since he gave up comics.

At school the idea of a band really takes off and lots of people want to join in. Rehearsals become big noisy affairs. I don't mind. I just love watching Ben with the kids, the way he gets them organised and the knack he has of making everyone feel part of the show. Miranda and Kerry-Ann become my backing singers and I spend ages teaching them the words to all the songs. They get themselves up like dogs' dinners in micro skirts and tiny crop tops and back-comb their hair into incredible shapes. Ben is amazing with the kids who want to play percussion, and gets them in a line with tambourines and triangles. Everyone who wants to gets a chance to play something.

In true Meadowlea tradition, the exams are just a passing inconvenience. I can't get worried or worked up about them now I have given up any hope of going to college. It is just a drag to sit for hours in a hot hall with Mr Backhouse walking up and down with a face like an undertaker. I am more concerned for Ginna, because he hasn't done any work at all, and sometimes I watch him fidgeting and looking out of the window, and I know that for him the questions might as well be written in Arabic.

Throughout this time I keep writing to Simon, who is still bombarding me with poems and chunks from Shakespeare. I don't know how he gets time to keep writing it all down. But there is so much I can't tell him. I hate Meadowlea and the stigma of being a pupil there. I can't wait to leave and be different. But part of me, the part that loves Ben, is just dying slowly day by day as the time to part comes closer.

I want to hold on to all the moments when we are together and keep them forever, but time goes by so fast... And I know that soon all I will have left is the baby photo and my memories.

Simon writes and asks me to go to a party with him when he is home for the weekend. I know I should refuse. I dread the thought of being with him, of him holding my hand and kissing me. But it seems mean to say no and I don't have anything else to do. So I write explaining that we have a dress rehearsal at school until eight but that I will meet him at my house at eight-thirty.

The dress rehearsal is a mess. The percussion kids make so many mistakes that even Ekky shouts at them. I sing flat and Ben keeps staring at me as if I'm an idiot. The worst thing is that Ginna doesn't turn up, so I have to try to play guitar and sing. Ben is furious with Ginna but I can see he is trying not to show it.

'I suppose it's impossible to expect professional standards from kids,' Ben says bitterly, his mouth a dejected moody line, as I hit yet another bum note.

At that moment the door bursts open and Ginna rushes in. 'He opened his eyes, he knew it was me. He squeezed my hand!' he shouts. And Ben gives this roar of approval and they rush and hug each other. I just stand, the guitar limp against my stomach, staring at them. We can share in the news but we are excluded from the magic circle of their spontaneous brotherly embrace.

As we are all leaving school, a red jeep streaks up the hill and stops in front of us. Simon jumps down and runs across to me, like some ardent lover from a film who can't wait to get to his girl. I spoil it by ducking away from his embrace.

'Hi, you're early,' I say without enthusiasm, and try to steer him back across the road to his car.

'Hi there. How ya doin'?' calls Miranda. She's boy crazy and *has* to talk to anything in trousers. Simon stops to front of her, and she and Kerry-Ann dissolve in giggles. 'Aren't you going to introduce us, Fawn?' Miranda says, with a pout and a wiggle of her hips.

Reluctantly I stop pulling at Simon's arm and say loudly: 'Everyone, this is Simon. Simon, this is Mr Thompson and the band: Ginna, Ekky, Miranda, Kerry-

Ann, Tariq, Pete, Ant and Mujat.' Desperately I grab Simon's arm and try to turn him around, but he is like a horse with its nose in a hay-bag and stays rooted to the spot.

'Very nice to meet you, Mr Thompson, sir,' he says, holding out his hand to Ben. 'Heard a lot about you from Fawn,' he adds smoothly.

Kerry-Ann's mouth has fallen open at this display of manners, the use of 'sir' and Simon's cut-glass voice. 'Bleeding 'ell,' she mutters. 'It's Prince Willie.'

'Pleased to meet you, Simon,' Ben says quietly. Then he looks across at the jeep with a frown and says: 'You'll take good care of Fawn, won't you?'

Simon's face darkens and his smile is rather forced as he says with an attempt at light-heartedness: 'I know Fawn's a star – I shall cherish her, I assure you.'

'I'm sure you will,' Ben says sternly, and he glances at me with a look of curiosity and disapproval which makes some tender part of me hurt like crazy. I don't know what I am more worried about – that Ben will think Simon the ultimate creep, or that he is a cool guy and wonder why he is going out with someone like me. Either way, I am furious with Simon for coming up to the school. I wanted to keep these different parts of my life separate. It's almost impossible to believe that there could be anything to do with school which is so precious I want to keep it secret – but now I know there is.

'Come on, let's go,' I mutter to Simon. And I begin to

walk across to the jeep so he has to follow. He is obviously cross because he pulls away from the pavement with a squeal of tyres.

'I thought you said he was old!' he says angrily.

'Who?' I ask, playing for time.

'That teacher – dear old Mr Thompson. I've been bored witless reading about him for weeks and then when I meet him I find he looks like bloody Michael Owen.'

'Do you think so?' I ask airily. 'And you should have told me my letters were boring,' I add, danger creeping into my voice. 'I wouldn't have bothered to write to you.'

'He's young and good-looking and you're obsessed with him,' Simon spits out. 'You've filled pages about him. What am I meant to think?'

'Oh I don't care what you think! Let me out! Go to this party on your own. I don't want to come!' I shriek at him.

'OK, I'm sorry.' His anger evaporates in the face of my obvious rage. 'It's just... I've told you how I feel about you, Fawn. And you've...' He stops. He obviously wants to tell me that my letters have been an immense disappointment to him but doesn't know how.

'Look, Simon. This is all much too heavy for me. We don't know each other. I'm not going to tell you things I don't feel or know for sure. Just take me home and let's forget all about it, shall we? And I shan't bore you with any more details of my life from now on,' I add bitterly.

'Look, let's start again, shall we? I'm desperate for my friends to meet you,' he says in a conciliatory tone.

'Everyone at school was knocked out by your photograph. They're dying to meet you.'

I tell myself I should feel flattered and not like some animal that has been bagged by a great white hunter. And I sit silently while he talks about school. His anger about Ben has burned painfully into my brain. Because I know he has spoken the truth. I *am* obsessed with Ben. I want all of him, all of the time. I don't want to share him with anyone or anything. Not even poor needy Spider. I am hungry for him constantly. And I wonder, when I am deprived of the sight and sound of him, if this hunger will eat me up from the inside. Eventually, I don't even hear Simon's words – they are just background noise to my thoughts about Ben.

The huge modern bungalow we arrive at is even bigger and posher than Simon's house. As we walk around the house I can see a swimming pool in the back garden, gleaming blue like a kingfisher's wing through the screen of bushes. It looks cool and inviting.

The boy who opens the door is shorter than Simon with an ugly, intelligent face and long golden-brown hair. He has kind brown eyes which I like. He looks at me with a big grin, takes a step back and whistles. 'Hi, my name's Nick. You must be the fantastic Fawn.' He turns to Simon and pretends to punch his shoulder. 'You did not lie, my son...'

He and Simon then pretend to have a fight and I stand, feeling hot and rather affronted. It gives me a creepy feeling to know that Simon has been talking about me to his friends, and I wonder what he's told them and how much is true. I bet he hasn't told them I go to Meadowlea.

'Come in and meet everyone,' Nick says, taking hold of my arm. He leads me into a vast sitting room. The carpet is navy blue and the sofas and chairs are white leather. I can't help thinking of Adam's mum and how she'd love it all, especially the crystal chandeliers.

Despite the grandeur of the house, it doesn't seem to be much of a party. There are five boys in the room and two girls. Nick introduces me to everyone in turn, as if I am the guest of honour. He keeps on telling me how glad he is that I could come, which is very nice. The boys – Joe, Paul, Rob, Laurie and David – all shout 'Hi' and smile at me and I begin to relax a little.

The girls are called Jane and Sarah and they look practically identical. Both have masses of long straight hair, which falls over their faces and has to be flicked back at intervals, like horses swishing their tails. Both wear little floral dresses with tiny rolled-ribbon straps. These dresses could almost be under-slips because they are so flimsy and skimpy, but the cut and the silkiness suggest they are very expensive. They both have long brown slender legs like gazelles and wear strappy high-heeled sandals. As Nick announces who I am and shouts out their names the girls both turn to stare at me without smiling. I am suddenly conscious of my hair and wish I had an elastic to tie it back.

Even though I am wearing my best skirt and a new top, which I bought specially for the gig, under the unwinking scrutiny of Jane and Sarah I suddenly feel scruffy. 'Hi,' I say, to try to fill the silence. 'Are you two sisters?'

They are immediately suffused in giggles, hiding their faces behind their hands like children. They look at each other and giggle some more. 'You look so alike,' I say lamely.

'Come on into the kitchen,' says Nick, taking hold of my arm. 'Let me find you a drink. There are some nibbles too.' He leads me into the kitchen, which is as beautiful as the rest of the house with decorated wall tiles and pine furniture. As I haven't eaten since lunch, I am pretty disappointed when I see the selection of nibbles. There are some crisps and peanuts in bowls and that's all. There is a very beautiful basket of fruit as well, but it is so carefully arranged I feel sure it is a decoration and you're not meant to help yourself.

'There's wine or beer,' Nick says. 'Or some fruit juice if you'd rather have that.'

'Yes, some fruit juice would be lovely, thanks,' I say, helping myself to a handful of crisps and thinking that juice might fill me up a bit.

He opens an enormous fridge and brings out a crystal jug full of pink liquid. He sniffs it tentatively. 'I'm not sure what it is – might be passionfruit.'

'Oh, great! Give her a big glass,' Simon jokes as he comes into the kitchen. He reaches for the opened bottle of wine on the table and pours out a glass.

'Is that for you?' I ask.

He nods and takes a sip.

'But you're driving!' I say indignantly.

Nick laughs and says: 'You two are sounding very married. Is there something you haven't told us, Simon, you old dog?'

'It's not bloody funny,' I say, taking the glass from Simon's hand. 'I don't want to end up being fed through a tube. If you want to drink, you can forget about taking me home.'

There is an ugly little silence between us. I had not realised before that when Simon frowns, his brows meet in a dark bad-tempered line across his forehead. Even though this is a lovely house and Nick is very sweet, I wish I hadn't come out with Simon again.

'And how exactly are you going to get home if I don't take you?' he says in a nasty patronising voice.

'This is Leeds, not Outer Mongolia. I'll get a bus. Like the rest of the world does,' I say rudely. And I pick up my bag from the kitchen table and make for the door. 'Thanks Nick, nice to have met you,' I say over my shoulder. Simon races after me, grabs hold of my arm and turns me back into the kitchen.

'Oh come on, Fawn. Don't go off in a huff, please. I'll drink passionfruit juice with you.' Nick laughs at this remark, pours another tumbler full of pink juice and winks at Simon, who slips his arm around my waist as he says: 'It'll be a fun evening. We can swim later.'

'You didn't say anything about swimming, I haven't brought anything...' I say, pulling away from him and returning to attack the crisps.

'Oh, Nick will find you a towel, won't you Nick?' Simon and Nick grin wolfishly at each other and I ignore them as I sip the juice and look around the kitchen.

Simon goes into the sitting room and leaves me alone with Nick. He smiles and says: 'Simon tells me you've just finished taking your GCSEs. What are you going to do next?'

'Get a job,' I say flatly.

'Really?' Nick sounds astounded. 'What kind of job?'

'Well, anything really. I'm going to study music later on, I hope. So I want to get some savings under my belt.'

'Music, how fantastic. Simon said you sing with a group.'

'Yeah, well it's the school band. But it's good fun.'

'So you're going to be a pop star, are you, Fawn?' Nick asks, with a smile.

'No. I don't think so. Eventually, I'd like to be a music teacher.' This idea, only half-formed until now, has been floating around in my mind for a while. The idea of studying at evening class and then going on to college. And then, one day, maybe meeting Ben again as an equal.

'Oh! That will be nice,' Simon says sarcastically. He has been standing in the doorway listening to me. 'Marvellous Mr Thompson has been inspirational, hasn't he?'

I turn on him in fury. 'Yes, as a matter of fact he has. He's someone who makes the world a better place just by being alive and the work he does is great. And yes, I would like to be like him. So what?'

'Hell!' Nick says, putting his hands over his ears. 'You two better kiss and make up. Come on, let's swim. I think you need cooling down.'

Nick takes my hand and leads me out to the poolside. The other kids come out too; they are holding glasses and laughing. Everyone is having a good time except me and Simon. I wish I hadn't come. It is terribly hot. The sun has disappeared and the sky has darkened, but the air is heavy and sultry. Soon it will start raining but now the air is suffocating.

There are sun loungers around the pool and piles of crisp towels on a low table. I sit on the edge of one of the loungers and finish my juice. My stomach is rumbling with hunger; the juice and crisps seem to have made it worse. I think about the bananas in the fruit bowl in the kitchen and crave for one.

To my astonishment Jane and Sarah slip off their sandals and then shimmy out of their dresses with little shakes of their hips and shoulders. The dresses fall to the ground in shiny heaps like two coiled snakes. They are both wearing tiny briefs and nothing else. I note, dispassionately, that Jane has heavier thighs than Sarah. Apart from that, their gleaming bodies, with pert breasts and long legs, are the same with an all-over suntan. They both dive into the pool and surface together to flick their hair back.

Simon grins at me. He is peeling off his top. 'Come on, Fawn. Are you coming in?' I look at him coldly. Up until now I have reserved judgement on him. Now I know I hate him.

'I can't swim,' I say. And I go back into the kitchen and pull a banana out of the immaculate fruit bowl and eat it.

Later Simon comes into the kitchen to find me. His hair is wet and he has a towel wrapped around his waist. 'What's the matter now, Fawn?' he says irritably. 'Surely the girls going topless didn't upset you? Everyone in continental Europe does it. Even the grandmothers!'

'Well I don't,' I say sulkily.

He sighs as if I am a difficult child having a tantrum. 'At least come and sit outside with us. It looks crazy you sitting in here on your own.'

'I want to go home,' I say miserably.

'OK, just give me half an hour. It's Nick's birthday and we've got a little present for him. Just come outside and join in the party, OK?'

Nick has lit scented candles to keep away the insects and the poolside has spheres of light and darkness. Deliberately I find a seat in the dark and sit down. I lean back and close my eyes. The air is full of waxy perfume and the chemical smell of swimming-pool water and the heat is almost unbearable. I can feel sweat under my arms and along my hair-line. And I realise I will have to wash my top tonight and hang it to dry in the bathroom so it will be clean for the gig.

Suddenly a smell I know only too well hits me like a cosh across the nose and I sit up immediately and look around, as wary as a guard dog. The others are huddled in a circle and I see Nick breathe deeply on a big hand-rolled cigarette and then hand it to Jane.

'Great present, folks,' he says as he exhales a plume of blue smoke into the night air. 'Marvellous idea. Something we can all share. Oh, Fawn! You are awake. Are you going to come over and have a drag?' he asks kindly.

Jane and Sarah both titter and Jane coughs a bit and hands the joint on to one of the boys. I stand up and pull my skirt down. I don't care if they do think I'm a drag. 'I don't take drugs,' I say loudly and clearly.

'Oh for crying out loud,' Simon says with a groan. 'It's less harmful than tobacco. It's a completely natural substance. I thought all you city kids were into it.'

'Well I'm not. I don't want to fry my brain,' I say truculently. Jane and Sarah laugh at this. I can't trust myself to say anything more so I march into the kitchen, get my bag, go through the front door and out into the gloom of the evening.

For all my brave words I haven't got a clue where I am or how to get back to the city centre. I wish I had taken more notice when Simon was driving here. I don't even know if I am walking in the right direction to get on to the main road. There is also the small problem that I have very little money on me, maybe not enough for a bus, even if I do manage to find one. To add to my discomfort there is a rumble of thunder and then raindrops, the size of ten-pence pieces, start to fall from the sombre night sky.

The rain has got really heavy and I am soaked before Simon comes to look for me. He leans over and opens the jeep door and says in a surly voice: 'Get in, for heaven's sake.'

It grieves me to do so. I wish I could walk off into the night and tell him to get lost, but the rain is like a cold torrent and my hair and clothes are sodden. My main concern is for my shoes, which are squelching as I walk. They are the only ones I have and I need them for the gig. So I get wearily into the jeep and sit and shiver on the seat. Simon is completely silent.

At last he says in this really hurt voice, 'You can have no feelings for me at all. If you did you would have made some effort to get on with my friends. You could have tried to join in – had a swim and smoked a little dope. Jane and Sarah only had a tiny puff each. Everyone else was having a really good time. But you are just so chippy and difficult!' His voice rises; he is getting cross now. 'And nothing bloody well suits you, does it? Not Italian food, or going to nice houses, nothing. You really are a drag, Fawn! You deserve to spend your life on some dreary council estate hiding behind dirty net curtains.'

'I don't intend to do that,' I say coolly. 'And I don't care what you think of me. I don't want to die young.'

'Don't be so ridiculous!' he yells at me. 'Having a glass of wine or a few puffs of dope isn't killing material. It's good fun. It's what everyone does. Do you live in the real world?'

'There are lots of different ways to die,' I say grimly. And I think of Spider lying with his broken body in a hospital bed, and Pa imprisoned in the house.

'Oh, very clever,' Simon scoffs. 'Been studying philosophy, have we?'

'Oh eff off!' I say rudely. I could tell him about how Pa started off with a bright future until he started playing games with drugs, but I can't bring myself to. I don't care much what happens to Simon. And I doubt he would listen to me even if I tried to explain to him. Life has always given him what he wants, so he assumes he will be one of the lucky ones who stays in control of the monster and rides it with pleasure. One thing is for sure. I won't be waiting around to find out if he falls off.

We have reached the top of the estate. The lights are against us. This gives me my opportunity to get away. I jump out of the jeep and dodge through the waiting traffic. Behind me I can hear him shouting my name, but the cars behind are tooting and he has to move on. It's good to run. The rain has made the night cool and my clothes are icy against my skin. Jogging as fast as I can in my sodden shoes I cut through the estate, taking all the short cuts, but even so Simon gets to the house before me.

He gets down from the jeep and stands in my way, blocking the space between the broken gate and the rickety fence. 'Fawn, I'm sorry. I shouldn't have said those awful things to you. It's only because I love you...' I have this awful feeling he is just about to cry, and I duck under his arm and push him away. As I march purposefully up the path I hear him say: 'Fawn...' and his voice *is* breaking now.

I turn on him as he follows me to the front door. 'My parents are in bed. My Pa is ill. Don't make a scene.'

'I didn't know your father was ill,' he whispers.

'He had one bad trip too many,' I whisper back. 'Just think on that, Simon. Next time you're experimenting.'

'Fawn! I'll do anything...' he says. Just for a moment pity overtakes any other emotion. But then cruelty steps in to take its place.

'Just leave me alone, Simon,' I say wearily, because I am suddenly bone-tired. 'I'll never fit into your world. And I don't want to. I'd rather be me. Goodbye.'

Closing the door on him, I lock it and then lean against it. He rings the bell a couple of times but I ignore it. Eventually I get fed up with standing there listening to his desperate whispers. So I go up to my room and sit in the dark until I hear the roar of the jeep's engine and I know he has gone. Then I pull off my soaking clothes and wrap myself in my bedspread to get warm.

After a time I go down to the kitchen and make tea and toast. The food makes me feel better, and when I have finished I start washing my clothes and stuffing my shoes with newspaper. I have to get ready for the gig. That is all I will allow myself to think about. Because tomorrow is the end of term. And after tomorrow I will be leaving Meadowlea and Ben for ever.

9

Nature is cheating on me when I open my eyes in the morning, it should be cold as midwinter, or pouring with rain, something in keeping with my black mood. Instead I find the thunderstorm has cleared the air and it is a bright, golden morning. Already I can feel the heat of the day starting to build as I slip out of bed and creep downstairs.

Ma has already gone to work, but Ginna is in the kitchen making tea and pouring enormous mounds of cereal into a bowl. 'Well, this is it,' Ginna grins. He cautiously sniffs at the bottle of milk on the table and decides to eat his cornflakes dry. 'Last day of school! Feels funny, doesn't it?'

We pour out the tea and drink it black with lots of sugar to make up for the milk being off. 'I expect it feels funny because we've become institutionalised. Like long-term prisoners,' I say gloomily.

'Yeah, well, I'm not going to miss school,' Ginna says, shovelling cereal into his mouth. 'I'm gonna help Mr Thompson with the silaging. And he says he'll help me find a full-time job.'

'Can't Mr Thompson give you a job?' I ask. A tiny fantasy, born in an instant, plays out like a film in my head. If Ginna works at the Thompsons' farm it would give me a link with Ben. A chance that I might hear what he was doing and have the possibility of meeting him. But Ginna's reply kills off any hope.

'Nope, he can't afford it. I wish he could, because Mr Thompson's great and Mrs Thompson's an ace cook.' Ginna stops eating for a moment and grins at me. 'And Ben Thompson's a good bloke. Best teacher we've ever had.'

'I suppose so.' My tone is carefully neutral. Having managed to keep my feelings a secret from Ginna I must be careful now, on this last day. I eat a small amount of dry cereal and then push the bowl away. The remainder will go to the rabbits and guinea pigs because we are not allowed to waste food no matter how bad we feel.

'What you gonna do now school is finished, Fawn?' Ginna frowns at me.

'I don't know. Get a job. Earn some money,' I say bleakly. I can't think any further than today. I can't even believe that tomorrow I will still be here, sitting in the kitchen, eating breakfast, talking to Ginna, knowing that I won't be seeing Ben again.

The memory of my childish tears over Adam comes into

my mind and it seems like part of my childhood – like the year I cried at Christmas because I didn't get a Tiny Tears doll in my stocking. Now the full weight of adult misery has washed me clean. I have gone beyond tears or even the strange numbness I felt after Adam. I am as cold and mechanical as a machine. And, like a robot, I rise to my feet and start to clear the table and wash the pots.

When I start to get ready for school I find my shoes are ruined – the soles have come away from the uppers. They were very cheap and now look like they were originally made from cardboard. Riffling through the kitchen drawer I find some super glue and a couple of clothes pegs and try to stick the soles back on.

Then I survey the horror that was my new top. Last night I must have skimped on the rinsing because soap is etched into the buttons and the material is a horrid grey colour instead of bright white. I keep thinking to myself that today is the last time I'll see Ben and I am almost paralysed with terror.

Pa comes into the kitchen when I am washing the top. He is wearing an old tartan dressing gown which Ma bought in the Oxfam shop and his hair is sticking up. He looks like a mad professor. 'What are you doing, Fawn?' he asks, peering into the teapot to see if there's any tea left.

'I need this top for school. I thought I'd wash it and hang it outside for a while,' I mumble.

Pa pours the dregs of cold tea into a mug and sips it. 'It won't dry in time for school,' he says, picking up one of my shoes from the chair and inspecting it. 'What's this, a science experiment?'

'My shoes got wet and now they've fallen to bits,' I say angrily, splashing myself with icy water as I rinse the top. I am on the verge of tears of temper and self-pity. 'It's our gig tonight,' I add.

Pa shakes his head and wanders out of the kitchen with his mug of tea. I finish rinsing the top and peg it out in the sunshine. Then I go up to the bathroom and wash my hair in cold water, shivering despite the warmth of the morning.

When I come out of the bathroom Pa is waiting on the landing for me. His face is all smiley and this alone makes me stop in my tracks.

'I've found you something lovely to wear, Fawn. I brought this back from Afghanistan for your Ma, and there are some sandals as well. You'll be the belle of the ball in these.' He sounds so happy and pleased with himself that I don't have the heart to tell him I would rather die than go on stage in some awful hippy relic.

'My top will be fine. It'll be dry by now. I'll run the iron over it,' I say hastily.

'Oh no,' Pa says, blocking my way. His face is all screwed up with pleasure and he holds the dress out to me. 'This is much better. And you're about the same size as Ma was at your age. Put it on, Fawn, please,' he urges.

'No...' I say miserably.

From downstairs Ginna calls: 'You gonna be all day, Fawn?'

'I haven't got time,' I plead, trying to dodge past Pa. But he will not budge.

'Just try it on, please, for me,' he says, as insistent as a child. And I don't have the heart to refuse.

The dress is long and baggy and made from some very fine fabric which reminds me of Jane and Sarah's shimmery little dresses. It is covered in rainbow embroidery and tiny glass beads. It is very pretty.

Slipping off my skirt and top I pull the dress over my head. A misty reflection, encircled in sun spots from the ancient mirror on Ma's dressing table, gazes unsmilingly back at me.

The dress is a little too big and slips over on to one shoulder exposing my collar bones. It is too long to be fashionable and reaches below my knees. But it feels wonderfully silky against my skin, and the fringing along the cuffs and hem brushes my bare legs and wrists as I move. This feeling reminds me of past pleasures: the first tingle of salt water when you run into the sea, or the feel of clean sheets on a bed.

I slip my feet into the soft blue leather sandals. Even if this outfit looks a little strange, it is better than my crinkly shoes and grey top. 'OK. I'll wear it,' I say, opening the door.

'Oh, Fawn! You look beautiful,' Pa says, his face beaming and sincere.

I surprise myself as I lean forward and give him a sudden hug. I can't remember the last time I touched him. He feels very bony and frail inside my arms, fragile and vulnerable like a bird or rabbit. 'Thanks for finding the dress for me, Pa,' I whisper. Then I hurry back into the room to get changed.

We don't have lessons on this last day. Instead, we are sent to the hall to help Ben. He has a student who is taking his classes so we can spend the whole day with him. It's brilliant. Not like school at all. Ben has his beat box playing music. And he has brought in a kettle, a stack of plastic mugs, hot chocolate and coffee, as well as tins of biscuits for us.

First we clear all the chairs from the hall and then we decorate the walls with streamers and posters. We stop for lots of coffee breaks and everyone helps and gets on together really well. There is no fighting or bawling and I can't help wondering why school couldn't have always been like this.

We fill a big net full of balloons and fasten it to the ceiling. It will be let down at the end of the evening as a grand finale. Then Ben gets big bits of paper from the art room and giant felt-tip pens and we all have to write a message or draw a little picture. These are going to be used to decorate the area behind the band, so it becomes a wall of graffiti.

Most people write goodbye, but I don't want to write that. I spend ages doing a picture. Then I write: *IT'S BEEN GOOD TO KNOW YOU ALL, love from Fawn*. Because anything else seems very final and I am not in the mood for endings at all.

By the middle of the afternoon we have finished the hall. We have one last cup of coffee and finish the biscuits. Then everyone but the band leaves and we begin our final rehearsal.

We are all a bit nervous and over-excited and everything goes wrong. We can't keep in time. We can't seem to play a tune together. And Miranda and Kerry-Ann can't remember the words to the backing vocals. Ben's face becomes tense as we carry on murdering the music. I start to feel sick with tension.

'Look, just relax everyone,' Ben finally says, pushing his hair back from his forehead. 'Girls, your dancing is brilliant,' he adds, smiling winningly at Miranda and Kerry-Ann. 'And if you forget the words to the songs, don't worry. It doesn't matter at all. But do Fawn a favour; don't make up any new ones, just lalala or mime. Fawn knows the words and she'll just carry on.' He turns to the percussion section. 'Ekky, can you get your lads bunched up a bit more so they can keep in time with you?'

I'm surprised he is so calm. I feel like pulling my hair out because the band sounds diabolical and I have been singing really badly.

'We'll break for an hour and then have a warm-up. You're all doing very well. Just smile if you make a mistake. I know it's not easy because we haven't been playing together for very long. Just remember – we're doing this for fun.'

Ginna, Ekky and I go to the chippy for our tea. We hang around outside the chip shop for a while, then go back to school.

When we get to the top of the hill we see a big grey van parked outside the gates with the words *Yorkshire Television* emblazoned on the side. For a moment my mouth is dry with panic. I wonder if some of the little kids have got into school and set fire to the hall or something like that. Then common sense tells me that the fire brigade and police would be here too. It *is* weird though, like a time warp or something, because Mr Backhouse is standing on the steps, just like old Bluebottle did, talking into a big furry mike.

We slip into school unnoticed and race down to the hall. Ben is testing the sound equipment. I hear his voice coming out of the loud speaker. 'Testing, testing. One two three...' When he sees us he grins. 'Well done. I'm pleased you've come back early. I've got some news – I hope you'll be pleased. The regional news programme wants to film the band.'

'Oh bleedin' hell!' Ginna says before he can stop himself. 'We sounded terrible at the rehearsal. The kids are all going to pieces with nerves already! They'll wet their knickers at the idea of going on the telly. It's a crap idea.'

I give him a shove in the back and hiss: 'Stop swearing, you eejit. There's not much Ben – I mean, Mr Thompson – can do if they're already here.' I smile at Ben. 'We'll just have to make the best of it, won't we?'

'Creep,' Ginna whispers to me.

Ben looks worried. 'Well, I think Ginna has a point. To be frank it wasn't my idea. Mr Backhouse...'

He stops because the sound of Mr Backhouse's thundering voice can be heard in the corridor. Mr Backhouse is one of those people who never talks when he can shout and never walks when he can stride. Now he enters the hall like an army tank and bears down on us. Behind him, almost running to keep up, is a boy dressed like a pixie in tight green trousers and a matching polo-neck. He has two nose-rings, dozens of earrings and lurid bleached hair, and even by Meadowlea standards he looks weird.

'This is Jazz,' Mr Backhouse booms at us. 'From the television company.'

'Pigging hell,' whispers Ginna. 'The Martians have landed.' Ekky begins to giggle and quickly turns it into a cough.

Mr Backhouse says firmly: 'You will give Jazz every assistance.'

The other kids arrive and we get changed into our smart clothes. We set up the instruments and Ben asks us which song we would like to play for the television company. There's quite a lot of shouting and arguing until we settle on *Yellow Submarine*, which is our finale. We have a run-through and it sounds all right. Not brilliant or anything, but OK for a bunch of kids in a school hall.

But then, Jazz brings the cameras and sound equipment in, and we do our first take. The presence of the cameras and mikes swinging around makes everyone go to pieces. The band just about stops playing at one point. Ekky misses his cue and we have no drums at all. So there is just Ginna, me and Ben trying to get through it.

Jazz comes across and begins to organise us. 'We'll try again with just the drums, Mr Teacher on keyboard, this boy on guitar and you, gorgeous girl, on vocals,' he says, grinning like a imp at me.

'What about us, the backing singers?' Miranda says. She doesn't catch on too quickly.

'Not this time, darling,' Jazz says, shooing her and Kerry-Ann off stage. 'We'll just get the song in the can and then you can come back.'

'Will we still be on the telly?' Miranda asks, and I can see her mouth pouting with emotion.

'I'm not singing on my own,' I say quietly to Jazz.

'You won't be on your own, petal. You've got Mr Teacher to sing with you. And very nice together you are,' Jazz says, without looking at me. He begins to move Ginna into centre stage. 'Now. It's camera one for the opening shot. Then, when the green light moves, look into camera two. Understand? We'll try it once more – from the top.'

'He's not called Mr Teacher!' I say with irritation.

'It doesn't matter, Fawn,' Ben says.

'It bloody does!' I shout. 'And if they want us on the telly they should have all of us. This isn't an audition. We're all in the band. We all should play. I've told you. I'm not singing on my own.'

'Oh, quite the prima donna, aren't we?' Jazz retorts.

'It's just not fair,' I reply mulishly.

'Fawn's got a point,' Ben says with a quiet nod, looking at the disappointed faces of the kids who have been excluded.

'This band isn't like the rest of school. It isn't about people being in or out – or good enough or not good enough.' I'm still protesting. 'We're all the same. And we've all worked towards doing this gig.'

'Pretty girl! You're talking rubbish. You're much better on your own!' Jazz says incredulously.

'Shame,' I say, narrowing my eyes at him. 'We stick together. You want us – you have all of us. Take it or leave it.'

Jazz whispers a couple of very ripe swear words under his breath, and then turns to Ben. 'What do you think, Mr Teacher?'

'I agree wholeheartedly with Fawn. She's put it more eloquently than I could have done. I suggest everyone comes back on stage and we have another try,' Ben says gently, and Jazz raises his eyes to heaven and runs his hands through his hair until it stands on end.

This time Ben gets everyone in position, so they can see him and be conducted through their part. Jazz watches him and rolls a cigarette, using loose tobacco and Rizla paper. When he's finished it's as thin as a matchstick and he pulls on it bad-temperedly, blowing smoke out through his nose like an angry dragon and scowling at us.

We get through the song and it isn't too bad. 'That'll do,' Jazz says, nipping out his cigarette and popping the dog-end back into his tobacco tin. He has lost patience with us and wants to leave.

'Thanks everyone, that was great!' Ben says, grinning at us all. I look across at him and our eyes meet and hold. 'Thanks, Fawn,' he says quietly. When I look into his blue eyes I feel as if I am drowning in them.

People start to drift into the hall. Ekky loads the CD player and Ginna takes first shift as DJ. I have three hours and ten songs left with Ben. 'First set in ten minutes,' Ben says.

I watch the clock at the back of the hall. It is the same clock I watched during exams, when each second seemed like a minute and every minute an hour. Now, because I want this evening to last forever, it is like everything is speeded up. Ten minutes pass in the blink of an eye. And the group gets ready to start.

The hall is pretty full; quite a few teachers and parents have come along and are standing at the back. Some of the first years are dancing in front of the stage, but most people are just standing around. It's so hot all the emergency fire doors are open and people wander in and out.

Ben walks to the front of the stage and suddenly the hall is silent. 'Good evening, everyone,' he says.

The first years chorus obediently: 'Good evening, Mr Thompson.' Mr Backhouse, who has positioned himself at the back of the hall, beams with pleasure at this example of new Meadowlea manners.

'It's great that so many of you have come along this

evening to support us. We are the school band. We don't have a name. We've been too busy rehearsing to think of one. We play all kinds of music. If you want to dance, or sing along, please do so. We are very lucky in having a singer who writes her own material and we would like to start this evening with a song she wrote called *Heartbreak*. Please give a warm welcome to Fawn McKenzie and the Meadowlea band.'

Everyone starts clapping and cheering and I get stage fright. I am frozen to the spot and I can't move my feet. It is as if Ben knows this because he walks over, takes hold of my hand, and leads me to the mike. The touch of his hand, warm and strong, is very comforting. It makes me feel wonderful. I bite my lip and look down at the floor. I am terrified everyone in the hall will see my feelings mirrored in my eyes. 'Fawn McKenzie,' Ben says again, just in case anyone doesn't know who I am.

Slowly, too slowly, the band starts the intro to my song. It is the easiest of all the songs we are doing which is why we are starting with it. But, even so, the percussion is all over the place and Ginna's guitar is twanging away as flat as a pancake. I close my eyes and try not to think of Ben.

When I open them I suddenly see Ma. She has come in through one of the fire exit doors and is standing at the side of the hall. She has washed her hair and put on her best jeans and T-shirt. I concentrate on her because I feel sure that if I look at Ben I will start to cry.

The band completely loses the tune after the first verse and I have to sing the chorus three times, with Ben valiantly keeping the harmony going, until they finally get it together and plunge me into verse two. I love verse two. It is my favourite.

There was a full moon rising in the sky
And the stars had come to light my way
When I saw you I forgot who I was
Yes I forgot who I was, 'cos I love you so.
It'll be heartbreak for me, I saw the signs
But this love won't go away, oh no,
This love won't go away.
I don't want to be happy, I don't want to be sad
I just want to be with you, yes, I want to be with you...

As I sing this song to the crowded hall, I realise it is just like the songs Pa has played over the years. And I wonder, for a faltering moment, if it really is corny old mush, like Ginna says. And maybe I have made a terrible mistake by ever letting anyone hear it. I am so taken up with this worry that I completely miss the chorus and the intro for verse three. Because I am not singing, there is a long musical solo which finally grinds to a halt.

I swallow hard, wondering if the group will realise that we haven't finished the song and start up again, but the audience don't give them time. They erupt into applause; even the little kids in the front are clapping hard. Mr

Backhouse is shouting 'BRAVO' very loudly and this embarrasses the hell out of me. I feel a hotness creeping up my neck. All I want to do is run off and into the small room behind the stage, but a quick glance around shows me the rest of the band grinning broadly, so I reckon I better not desert them.

'Thank you very much,' I say into the mike. I catch glimpse of Ma's face and she is grinning like a Cheshire cat. 'Our next song...'

My voice trails off because behind Ma I can see a shadowy figure. Someone tall and thin standing half in, half out of the doorway as if getting ready to flee. My first thought is that I am imagining things – it cannot be Pa. But then I see Ma turn, smiling and nodding. I catch a glimpse of a halo of thin grey hair, the pale shadow of a bearded face, the outline of faded jeans and a black leather waistcoat. Then I know a miracle has happened.

'This next song is dedicated to my Pa,' I say very firmly. Looking up I see Ben's smile. 'It was the first song I remember hearing when I was a kid. *Three Steps to Heaven.*' The crowd claps again, which is just as well because Ekky and his percussionists start off on a reggae beat instead of rock beat. Ben and I plug away with the tune until everyone else catches on and then I begin to sing.

Pa and Ma disappear after that song, so by the end of our first session I am convinced I have imagined the whole episode.

'Did you see Pa?' I ask Ginna, as we swig orange squash and eat biscuits. Ekky is being DJ and everyone else is shouting and laughing. They are all as high as kites with adrenaline from the gig. I feel like a ghost: here but not here.

'Nah! It wasn't him,' Ginna says. 'Can't have been.'

Ben is suddenly next to me. 'Did you see your father?' he asks quietly, so his words are not overheard by anyone else.

'Yes... How?' I stutter.

'I sent a taxi for him. I thought he should hear you sing, Fawn. And see how good Ginna is on the guitar.'

'He came in a taxi?' Ginna says in astonishment.

'Yes, the taxi driver is a friend of mine. I arranged for him to wait outside so your Dad could stay as long as he wanted and could get home straight away. I don't think it was easy for your Dad.' Ben looks into our faces and frowns with the effort of finding the right words. 'But he really wanted to see you both on stage. And I hope it might have helped him.'

'Yeah, thanks,' Ginna says slowly. I can't speak. I simply nod my agreement and Ben moves away.

After the disco finishes the band stays behind to tidy away. Finally everyone leaves until there is just Ginna, Ben and me. Just like it was in the beginning when the group was first formed.

'Well, I think we've put Meadowlea on the map tonight,' Ben says with satisfaction. He and Ginna laugh together, pleased and happy that it's all over and has gone well.

'Would you two like a lift home?' Ben asks kindly.

'Yeah, great. I've got to be up at the crack of dawn to help your dad,' Ginna says, yawning.

'Come on then, let's get you home to bed. I think Fawn's tired too,' Ben adds.

I am not suffering from tiredness. I am dying from despair. When we get to our house, I look along the narrow street of scruffy houses and I wish I was someone else. Anyone. It wouldn't matter. I just don't want to be me with all this anger and pain inside me.

'Have a good summer. I'll see you soon,' Ben says. He suddenly seems tense and tired. I get the feeling he wants to be rid of us. Ginna stops and leans into the car.

'You have a good time. You're off to Greece, aren't you?'

'Yes, five weeks in the sun. Should be good,' Ben says rather abruptly. 'Take care, both of you.'

Then he is gone. Those are his last words to me. And they weren't even to me. They were to both of us. For the first time in my life I really resent Ginna.

'Why didn't you tell me Ben was going to Greece?' I ask explosively.

'He's going island-hopping with a friend from university.' Ginna is walking up the path, unaware of my rage.

'How do you know? Is he going with a girl? And why didn't you tell me before?' I am following him, my voice an angry whisper. I feel wild with jealousy.

'Mrs Thompson told me. And he's going with a mate called Ed. Not that it's any of your business. Why the hell should you care? What's it to you if he goes to the moon and back?'

'Oh, get lost!' I spit at him.

'Oh bleedin' hell! You're not going to tell me... You're not sweet on him, are you Fawn?'

'NO! No, I'm not sweet on him!' I am as taut and edgy as an angry she-cat. And in truth, 'sweet' is not a word I could use to describe my emotions towards Ben. If anything I feel angry with him because he's caused all this burning emotion and then disappeared from my life. I know it's not his fault. But love is not a rational emotion, and the anger you feel when parted from the one you love is not rational either.

I sit slumped at the kitchen table. Ginna feels sorry for me. He doesn't say another word about Ben and makes me a mug of cocoa. Then he goes to bed, leaving me alone.

Postscript

I spend the summer working in the supermarket. I do extra shifts and work on Sundays too. Ginna works every day as well. He does six days on a Government scheme and then helps Mr Thompson on his day off. Ma says we are workaholics. But we earn enough to buy Ginna a Honda 50 so Ma can have her bike back.

We take one day off and go to visit Spider. I can cope now because he has been moved to a home up in the Dales, where he has his own room and is looked after by nuns. It's a lovely place which smells of lavender polish and hot meals. Spider gets into trouble for speeding down the long corridors in his wheelchair and doing V signs at the Mother Superior, so I guess he's getting better. He doesn't talk too well apart from some guttural sounds, but he seems very pleased to see us.

We take Spider outside and push him around the grounds and feed the tame squirrels. The nuns are very kind and give us cola and biscuits on a tray and we sit under a huge copper beech tree and tell Spider about the gig and our jobs. We stay for most of the afternoon and when it's time to leave Spider seems sad. You could almost imagine tears in his eyes.

'I expect Ben will come and see you when he's back from Greece,' I say. And the look of delight in Spider's eyes reminds me of myself.

Suddenly, on impulse, I bend over him and kiss his cheek. The nuns keep him very clean and he smells of baby shampoo. When I move back I see his mouth working. His tongue flaps, like a small red fish, and then he manages to mutter: 'Fanks...'

'There,' Ginna says as we walk back to the bus stop. 'That wasn't too bad, was it? I think old Spider was really made up to see you, Fawn.' But I can't answer or I will start to cry. I never felt more sorry for Spider than I do now. Because I know we both love Ben in our own way.

Apart from visiting Spider I don't go anywhere or do anything. One strange discovery I make is that having a broken heart makes you hugely attractive to the opposite sex. I get asked out lots of times. The trainee manager at work, who is really cute and very popular, asks me for a date so often it gets embarrassing. Some times I wonder why I don't just say yes. But I am sick and cold inside and the idea of going out with a boy makes me feel weary.

The other girls at the supermarket think I'm odd. They feel sorry for me and suggest double dates and trips to the cinema. I can't be bothered with any of it. Instead, after work, I go home and write songs. I've got a folder full of them. It is when I think about how there is no one to show them to that I am really sad.

I know that Ginna sees Ben sometimes at the farm, but

my pride will not let me ask too many questions and so I live in a kind of suspended animation. All I do is wonder and dream about him, until sometimes he seems more real to me than the people around me.

Autumn arrives early; the leaves begin to change colour and the weather becomes wet. It rains every day. The schools are back and I know that Ben will be at Meadowlea. I have to stop myself from walking up there to try to catch a glimpse of him. It's just as well I work such long hours and get so tired.

I do know that Ginna has told Ben where I work, so I spend my time dreaming he will come into the store to see me. I re-run a scene with us meeting many times in my head, with all kinds of different variations. So I am not at all surprised when Vita, who works on the check-out next to mine, comes rushing over during my coffee break and says: 'There's a bloke downstairs, asking for you. He's waiting by your till.' She adds gleefully: 'He's ever so nice...'

Walking down to the store I'm in a trance-like state, joy mingled with fear. I have wished so hard for this moment I can't believe it's happening now. All this emotion turns to anger when I see Nick leaning against the sweet stand, reading Woman's Circle. He is wearing scruffy denims and his hair needs cutting.

'Are you going to buy that magazine?' I ask, as I open up my till with a crash.

He seems oblivious to the fact that I am just about to detonate with rage and disappointment and carries on grinning at me. 'Yeah, I'll take it for my mum. And these things, please Fawn.'

'How did you know I worked here?' I ask, through gritted teeth.

'Simon told me. He's gone up to Oxford, you know.'

I give a bored kind of shrug to show I couldn't care if Simon had gone to Mars. I bleep Nick's packet of biscuits and tins of beans and refuse to look at him.

'I'm at the University here, I've got a flat up the road,' he says chattily. I don't reply. 'Are you still singing?' he asks.

'No.'

'Are you studying music?'

'In the evenings,' I snap.

'Would you like to come out one evening, when you're not studying?' he asks. 'There are some good bands on in the Uni bar.'

'No, thanks,' I say, shoving all his stuff into a carrier bag. He doesn't seem to realise he has to pack up his stuff and let me get on with serving other people. I hand the bag to him. I feel like throwing it at him. He seems taken aback by my sharp refusal and the waves of raw rage that are radiating from me. 'Money?' I say sharply, holding out my hand to him.

He leans over towards me, so our faces are very close. His big brown eyes are puzzled and upset and his crooked face is all frowny and concerned. 'I'm not a creep like Simon,' he says softly.

'I thought he was your big mate,' I snarl back.

'He used to read your letters out loud to me...' Nick avoids my eyes. I throw his change at him. 'I'll see you around, Fawn,' he adds.

'Not if I see you first,' I mutter.

The next time he comes in, we carry on our conversation as if there hasn't been a break of nearly a week.

'Why on earth did you listen?' I hiss at him, as I stuff dried pasta and biscuits into a plastic bag. 'I think that's a really creepy thing to do. You could have walked out of the room or told him to stop!'

He takes hold of the bag and our fingers briefly tangle. I move back as if he is contaminated. He looks all shamefaced and goofy. He has such a funny face that I have to pretend to be stern. 'Well?' I say as if I am a school teacher.

'I liked to hear it all. It was wonderful being transported into your world. It was such fun... I always knew when he started to make it up. It wasn't your voice any more.' He looks away and says, 'I am sorry, Fawn. It didn't seem so wrong then, but after I met you...' He looks uncomfortable. 'Are you still in love with that Mr Thompson? Is that why you won't come out with me?'

'I won't go out with you because I don't want to,' I say.

'I'll see you,' he says gloomily.

After that he comes into the supermarket regularly for his shopping. He always waves and says 'Hi' but doesn't bother to come to my till and doesn't suggest we go out.

I try to find some of my initial indignation and anger every time I see him – but eventually I run out of steam. So he and Simon used to read my letters together, so what? I remember his brown eyes and how he tried to be kind to me at that awful party and begin to feel a bit sorry I've been so nasty to him. A couple of times I smile at him when he is passing, just to let him know I'm not a complete cow.

It's nearly Christmas when he speaks to me again. We are just closing. The cleaners have started to work at the far end of the store and the lights are slowly being put out.

'You're just in time. More beans... You should buy shares in Heinz,' I say with a smile.

'Fawn.' He isn't smiling, his face is very serious. 'My parents are coming over at the weekend. We are going to the theatre on Saturday night. We have a spare ticket. Will you come with us? Please. It's a wonderful musical about twins. I think you'll love it.' He swallows hard and tried to smile at me. A small wave of emotion hits me. I think it's pity.

'There must be loads of girls at the University – ask one of them,' I say kindly, as if he is a child. 'You don't want to take me out with your parents...' I stop. The whole idea is just too stupid for words.

'Fawn, I do.' He pushes his hair back from his forehead and grins at me. I find myself smiling back. 'I want to prove to you that I really am nothing like Simon. Come and meet my folks. I've told them all about you...'

'Do you have to wear special clothes to the theatre?' I ask suspiciously.

He shakes his head, his face ablaze with happiness. He is one of those people who can't hid their feelings, everything shows up in his eyes and his smile. 'I'll pick you up at about seven, OK? Look, here's my phone number if there's a problem. But please come.'

'OK,' I say, pocketing the piece of paper and smiling at my next customer.

Nick's parents are really nice and down-to-earth. His dad has the same rugby player-type face as Nick and his mum is very ordinary with grey hair. They make a big fuss of me as if I am a really special guest. We sit in a box at the theatre which is truly amazing – I feel like royalty.

The play is fantastic, but I am unprepared for the fact that as soon as it starts tears well in my eyes and begin to roll down my cheeks. There is nothing I can do to stop them. The play is so sad. It is the story of twins who are separated at birth because the mother can't afford to keep them both. I keep thinking how awful it would have been if Ginna and I had been parted. Nick is kind about my tears. He hands me tissues and pats my hand. And at the interval he touches my arm and says: 'I'm so pleased you're enjoying it, Fawn.'

Rubbing my eyes I say: 'I didn't know there were plays like this, about ordinary people.'

'Come on, let's go and have a drink. My parents are Friends so we don't have to queue in the bar; there's a private room.'

'I ought to go and wash my face. Has my mascara run?' I ask him.

He licks a bit of tissue and rubs under my eyes gently. 'All gone, and you look beautiful.'

It is only when we get into the function room that I realise we are holding hands. His dad gives us champagne in glasses with green stems. I start to feel a little fizz of happiness inside me as I sip it. This is the first time I have been out since the gig.

It is while I am in this little bubble of happiness, with the music still whirling in my head, that Ben appears in front of me from nowhere. In all the dreams and schemes I made up in my head, there was never anything like this. Nick and his dad are getting us something to eat so I am standing alone with Nick's mum. My legs go weak and I find I am leaning against her, like a wary child clinging to its mother.

Ben stops in his tracks at the sight of me. Then there is a small tentative smile that doesn't give anything away. The woman next to him is moving restlessly, but he ignores her. 'How are you, Fawn?' he asks.

'Fine...' I whisper, holding my glass so tightly I expect the fragile stem to shatter.

'I hear you've started your music course. That's good.' I am gazing at his face with the intensity of someone taking photographs of a vision. I briefly register that the woman with him has long hair and a plain face. And that he looks tired and older than I remember. Oh, dear God, please don't let Meadowlea be too much for him. I silently pray to any god who might be listening.

'This is Mr Thompson. My music teacher from school. From my old school,' I explain to Nick's mum. 'This is Mrs Mycroft, my friend's mum. This is the first time I've been to the theatre,' I add.

He smiles at me then, that old Ben smile, and my heart begins to melt. 'Well, we'd better go and get our drinks. Pop up to school sometime soon and let me know how you're getting on.'

Then he is gone, disappearing into the press of people, and with him go all my hopes and desperate, secret imaginings. I know in one clear moment that he will never love me. Not in the way I love him.

Nick's mum smiles at me. 'Well, that was a bit of surprise, wasn't it?' she says.

'Yes, I was crazy about him,' I whisper. As I say the words I realise two things. One, I have been able to tell someone other than Ginna the truth at last, and secondly I have used the past tense.

'Oh dear,' she says sympathetically. 'First love can be very painful. But you will get over it. I promise.' She squeezes my arm comfortingly.

'Oh! I don't want to get over it,' I whisper back to her. 'I want to remember it forever. I don't want the pain to ever go away. It was the most wonderful time of my life. He changed my whole existence. Nothing would be the same in my world if I hadn't met him. I want to love him for the rest of

175

my life.' I look down into my empty glass, wondering if it is the champagne which has loosened my tongue.

She laughs. She isn't embarrassed or anything – we are like two schoolgirls sharing a secret. 'Well, if you feel like that I'm sure he will be a great inspiration to you.'

'Yes,' I say. I want her to understand. 'He changed things for everyone,' I add. 'We were all kind of lost and alone, desperate for somewhere that was safe. And then he came along.'

'And now you're strong enough to stand alone,' she says gently.

Searching through the sea of faces I see Nick weaving through the crush. He is frowning with concentration, a tray in his hands. I find myself smiling at the sight of him. I think of how much I like him – of Pa going down to the allotment again – of Ginna working at the farm – and of Ekky, playing with an Indie band at the weekends.

'Yes,' I nod. 'Now we're all strong enough to stand alone.'